Praise for

Heritage

"*Heritage* shimmers off the page. The reader is seduced by three generations of the remarkable Lonsonier family, whose tales of anguish and love are echoed in the enchanting aviary they create in their garden in the Andes. The luminous characters endure passion and heartbreak through two world wars and beyond, with a plot that moves back and forth across continents. Translated exquisitely into English with beauty and precision, Bonnefoy's bold and magical book is a triumph."

—Patty Dann, author of *Mermaids* and *The Wright Sister*

"*Heritage* is a lyrical fever dream of a novel. By turns tender and ferocious, meditative and searing, it traces a graceful, looping line across history and generations, in the process laying bare the shared dreams, joys, and traumas that connect us as human beings. I loved it."

—Jennifer Cody Epstein, *USA Today* bestselling author of *Wunderland*

"Rich, evocative, charming, and quite simply stunning. In these poetically written pages following a single family, Miguel Bonnefoy's *Heritage* manages to speak volumes about history, courage, and home."

—Meg Waite Clayton, *New York Times* bestselling author of *The Last Train to London*

Heritage

Miguel Bonnefoy

Translated from the French
by Emily Boyce

Other Press
New York

First published in France in 2020 as *Héritage*
by Éditions Payot & Rivages, Paris.
Copyright © Éditions Payot & Rivages, 2020
Published by special arrangement with Éditions Payot & Rivages in conjunction
with their duly appointed agent 2 Seas Literary Agency.

English translation copyright © Gallic Books, 2022
First published in Great Britain in 2022 by Gallic Books, London.

Production editor: Yvonne E. Cárdenas
This book was set in Fournier MT Pro.

10 9 8 7 6 5 4 3 2 1

Library of Congress Cataloging-in-Publication Data
Names: Bonnefoy, Miguel, 1986- author. | Boyce, Emily, translator.
Title: Heritage / Miguel Bonnefoy ; translated from the French
by Emily Boyce.
Other titles: Héritage. English
Description: New York : Other Press, [2022] | First published in France
in 2020 as Héritage by Éditions Payot & Rivages, Paris
Identifiers: LCCN 2021056062 (print) | LCCN 2021056063 (ebook) |
ISBN 9781635421828 (paperback ; acid-free paper) |
ISBN 9781635421835 (ebook)
Subjects: LCGFT: Novels.
Classification: LCC PQ2702.O556 H4713 2022 (print) |
LCC PQ2702.O556 (ebook) | DDC 843/.92—dc23
LC record available at https://lccn.loc.gov/2021056062
LC ebook record available at https://lccn.loc.gov/2021056063

For Selva,
the only one who knows what happens next

Those who cannot remember the past are condemned to repeat it.
George Santayana

Lazare

Lazare Lonsonier was reading in the bath when news of the outbreak of the First World War reached Chile. In those days, he would often leaf through French newspapers at a 12,000-kilometer distance as he soaked in water infused with lemon peel. Later, when he returned from the front with half a lung, having lost two brothers to the trenches of the Marne, the scent of citrus would be forever associated in his mind with the stench of shells.

According to family legend, his father had left France with thirty francs in one pocket and a vine stock in the other. Born in Lons-le-Saunier in the foothills of the Jura, he had been the owner of a six-hectare estate when the wine blight hit, withering his vines and driving him to ruin. In the space of a few months, all that remained of four generations of winegrowing were dead roots in the apple orchards and wild plants from which he made a dismal absinthe. He left this land of chalk and cereal, morels and walnuts to board an iron ship at Le Havre bound for California. Since the Panama Canal was yet to open, he had to go the whole way round South America, traveling for forty days on a Cape Horner, aboard which two hundred men were crammed into cargo holds filled with caged birds, and the noisy fanfare was such that he didn't get a wink of sleep until the coast of Patagonia.

One night when he was wandering like a sleepwalker between berths, he saw an old, yellow-lipped woman with bracelets all the way up her arms and star tattoos on her forehead, sitting in the darkness on a rattan chair. She beckoned him towards her.

"Can't you sleep?" she asked.

She took from her bodice a small green stone pitted with tiny twinkling holes, no bigger than an agate bead.

"It's three francs," she said.

He paid, and the old woman burned the stone on a tortoiseshell which she waved under his nose. The rush of smoke went straight to his head and he thought he would faint. That night, he slept for forty-seven hours, a deep, unshakeable sleep filled with dreams of sea creatures swimming through golden vines. When he awoke, he threw up the entire contents of his stomach and he felt so heavy he could not get out of bed. He never knew if it was the old Roma woman's fumes or the fetid reek of the birdcages, but he sank into a delirious fever as they crossed the Strait of Magellan, hallucinating amid the cathedrals of ice, watching his skin become covered in gray patches as if turning to ash. The captain, who had learned to recognize the early signs of black magic, took one look at him and saw an epidemic looming.

"Typhoid fever," he declared. "We'll leave him at the next port."

This was how he found himself in Valparaíso, Chile, in the middle of the War of the Pacific, in a country he could not have placed on a map and of whose language he was utterly ignorant. On his arrival, he joined the long queue snaking from the fish warehouse to the customs post. Having realized that the immigration officer was asking each passenger the same two questions before stamping their forms, he concluded that the first must concern where the passenger had come from and the second his or her destination.

When he reached the front of the queue, the officer asked, without looking up: "*Nombre?*"

Not understanding a word of Spanish, but convinced of having guessed the question correctly, he responded without hesitation, "Lons-le-Saunier."

The officer's face was expressionless. Slowly, wearily, he noted down: Lonsonier.

"*Fecha de nacimiento?*"

"California," he replied.

The officer shrugged, wrote down a date and handed over the form. And so it was that this exile of the vineyards of the Jura was rechristened Lonsonier and was born a second time on May 21, the day of his arrival in Chile. Over the course of the next century, he never did continue his journey north, discouraged as much by the Atacama Desert as by the words of witch doctors, so that he sometimes said, as he gazed towards the Andes, "Chile has always reminded me of California."

Lonsonier soon became used to the reversal of the seasons, to midday siestas and his new name which, despite everything, still sounded French. He learned to feel an earthquake coming and in no time was thanking God for everything, good or bad. Within a few months he spoke as if he had been born in the region, rolling his "r"s like stones in a river, though a trace of an accent gave him away. As he had been taught to understand the constellations of the zodiac and to measure astronomical distances, he could decipher this new writing of the southern skies, with its fugitive star algebra, and understood that he had settled in another world of pumas and araucarias, a primeval world peopled with stone giants, willows and condors.

He was taken on as head grower at the Concha y Toro wine estate and set up several wineries called *bodegas* on the farms of llama and goose breeders. The venerable French vine claimed a second lease of life on the skirts of the cordillera, on the long, narrow strip of land which hung from the South American continent like a sword from a belt, a land where the sun shone blue. He soon joined a circle of French expatriates, transplanted and *chilianisés*, who had made smart matches and made their fortune in the foreign wine trade. Lonsonier, the humble winegrower, the simple countryman who had taken the road into the unknown, had suddenly become a shrewd businessman running several estates. From then on nothing – neither war nor blight, revolt nor dictatorship – could threaten his newfound prosperity, and as he marked the end of his first year in Santiago, Lonsonier blessed the day a Roma woman on an iron ship had burned a green stone beneath his nose.

He married Delphine Moriset, a waifish, delicate woman with straight red hair, who came from an old family of umbrella merchants from Bordeaux. Delphine would tell how her family had decided to emigrate to San Francisco after a drought in France, hoping to open a shop in California. The Morisets had crossed the Atlantic, sailed the coasts of Brazil and Argentina and passed through the Strait of Magellan before the ship called at the port of Valparaíso. It just so happened to be raining that day. Her father, the decisive Monsieur Moriset, walked onto the quay and within an hour had sold all the umbrellas he had brought on the journey in great sealed trunks. They never reboarded the ship for San Francisco and set up permanent home in this drizzly land sandwiched between mountain and ocean, where it was said that in some regions the rain could fall for half a century.

Brought together by twists of fate, the couple went to live in Santiago in an Andalusian-style house on Calle Santo Domingo, near the river Mapocho, whose waters swelled with the melting snows. The front of the house was screened by three lemon trees. The high-ceilinged rooms boasted Empire-era wicker furniture from Punta Arenas. In December, they had French specialities delivered, and the house was filled with boxes of pumpkins and veal *paupiettes*, cages of live quail, and plucked pheasants already displayed on silver platters, their flesh so toughened by the journey that it was hard to cut into them. The women would conduct incredible culinary experiments which seemed closer to sorcery than gastronomy. They mixed the age-old traditions of French cooking with the produce of the cordillera, filling the corridors with mysterious smells and clouds of yellow steam. They served empanadas stuffed with *boudin, coq au malbec, pasteles de jaiba* with morels, and reblochons so smelly the Chilean servants thought they must be made from the milk of sick cows.

Their children, who hadn't a drop of Latin American blood in their veins, were more French than the French. Lazare Lonsonier was the first of three boys born in bedrooms with red sheets which smelled of *aguardiente* and snake oil. Despite growing up surrounded by old women speaking Mapuche, their mother tongue was French. Their parents had not wanted to refuse them the heritage they had clung to along their journey, a legacy saved from exile. The French language was a kind of secret refuge, a code they shared, both a relic and badge of victory from a former life. On the afternoon of Lazare's birth, after his baptism under the lemon trees at the front of the house, they all processed into the garden and, dressed in white ponchos, celebrated by planting out the vine stock that Lonsonier senior had kept alive with a handful of soil inside a hat.

"Now," he said, packing down the earth around the stem, "we have properly put down roots."

From then on, despite the fact young Lazare Lonsonier had

never set foot in France, it became the focus of his wildest flights of fancy, as the chroniclers of the Indies must have imagined the New World. He spent his youth in a world of magical faraway stories, sheltered from wars and political upheaval, drawn to France by a siren-like call. To his mind, the French empire had so perfected the art of refinement that no account of it could ever do it justice. Distance, time and the lifting of roots had glorified the land his parents had bitterly left behind, so that he longed for a France he had never seen.

One day, a young neighbor with a German accent asked him which region his surname was from. The blond, well-dressed boy was descended from German settlers who had arrived in Chile twenty years earlier, his family having headed south to work the hard lands of Araucania. Lazare went home with the boy's question burning on his lips.

That same evening, his father, mindful of the fact his family had taken its name from a misunderstanding at a customs post, whispered in his ear: "When you go to France, you'll meet your uncle. He'll tell you everything."

"What's his name?"

"Michel René."

"Where does he live?"

"Here," he replied, placing a finger over his heart.

The traditions of the old continent were so deeply engrained in the family that come August, no one was surprised when they adopted the fashion for baths. Monsieur Lonsonier came home one afternoon with opinions on domestic cleanliness and imported the latest model of enameled cast-iron bathtub standing on four bronze lion feet, which had neither taps nor plughole, but was shaped like a pregnant woman's belly, with space enough for two people to lie side by side in the fetal position. Madame was impressed, the children giggled at its size and their father told them it was made of elephant tusks, proof that what lay before them was surely the most captivating discovery since the steam engine or the camera.

To fill the bath, he called for Fernandito Bracamonte, *el aguatero*, the neighborhood water carrier and father of Hector Bracamonte, who, some years later, was to play a decisive role in the family destiny. Fernandito was already as bent as a birch branch, with the enormous hands common to his trade. He would cross the city on a mule, carting barrels of hot water and carrying them upstairs to fill basins, his tiredness showing. He talked of being the eldest of many siblings on the Caribbean side of the continent, including the gold-digger Severo Bracamonte; a church restorer in San Pablo del Limón; a utopian from Libertalia and a *maracucho* journalist who answered to the name of Babel Bracamonte. Yet despite having many brothers, nobody seemed to care about him on the night the firemen found him drowned in the back of a tanker.

The tub was placed in the center of the room and, as each Lonsonier took turns to bathe in it, they added lemons from the porch to purify the water, and a bamboo bath rack on which to rest their newspaper.

Which is why, in August 1914, when news of the outbreak of the First World War reached Chile, Lazare Lonsonier was reading in the bath. A pile of newspapers had all arrived on the same day, two months late. *L'Homme Enchaîné* published Wilhelm II's telegrams to the Tsar. *L'Humanité* broke the news that Jaurès had been murdered. *Le Petit Parisien* gave information on the general state of siege. But the headline of the most recent edition of *Le Petit Journal* announced, in big, menacing characters, that Germany had just declared war on France.

"*Pucha*," he muttered.

The news brought home the distance between him and the land of his fathers. He was suddenly struck by a sense of belonging to this faraway country whose borders were being attacked. He leapt from his bath and despite the small, skinny, innocuous-looking body he saw in the mirror, a body ill-equipped for combat, he felt a surge of heroism rush through him. He pumped his muscles, and a simple pride warmed his heart. He felt he could hear his ancestors whispering to him and knew right away, with a tinge of fear, that he must respond to the call of destiny which, for a generation, had pitched his family towards the ocean.

He tied a towel around his waist and went down to the living room with the newspaper in his hand. With his family assembled in front of him, amid the thick scent of citrus, he raised his fist and declared: "I'm off to fight for France."

Memories of the War of the Pacific remained raw. The ongoing Tacna–Arica question, concerning provinces Chile had won from Peru, still led to flare-ups in the border regions. The Peruvian army having been trained by the French, and the Chilean army by the Germans, it was not difficult for the children of European immigrants born on the slopes of the cordillera to see parallels between the tensions in Alsace-Lorraine and those of Tacna–Arica. The three Lonsonier brothers, Lazare, Robert and Charles, unfurled a map of France on the table and began studying troop movements in meticulous detail (despite having no idea what they were looking at), convinced that their uncle Michel René was already out fighting in the Forest of Argonne. Having forbidden the playing of Wagner in their living room, they sat in the lamplight, piscos in hand, taking turns to name rivers, valleys, towns and hamlets. In the space of a few days, they had covered the map with colored drawing pins, tacks and little paper flags.

The servants watched this pantomime with dismay, respecting their orders not to lay the table while the map was out, and nobody in the household could understand how you could go and fight for a region in which you did not live.

And yet in Santiago, the call to war sounded as loudly as if it were coming from just next door, and soon people talked of little else. Out of nowhere another kind of liberty – freedom of choice, of homeland – was all around them, making its presence and its glory felt wherever you looked. Notices of conscription and fundraising efforts were pinned to the walls of the consulate and the embassy. Special newspaper editions were hastily printed and girls who spoke only Spanish were making boxes of chocolates in the shape of kepis. A French aristocrat living in Chile offered a 3,000-peso reward for the first Franco-Chilean soldier to be decorated for bravery. Lines of volunteers formed on the main roads and the boats began to fill up with recruits, the sons and grandsons of settlers heading off to join the ranks, faces brimming with confidence, bags filled with neatly folded clothes and carp-scale amulets.

It was such an alluringly cheerful sight that it was impossible for the three Lonsonier boys to resist the burning desire to sign up along with all the others, swept up in the pomp and pageantry. In October on La Alameda, the main avenue in Santiago, in front of a crowd of four thousand people, they joined the eight hundred Franco-Chileans boarding trains at Mapocho station for Valparaíso, where they were to embark on a ship bound for France. A mass was held at the church of San Vicente de Paul, between Calle 18 de Septiembre and San Ignacio, and a military band played a booming rendition of the Marseillaise before the tricolor flag. Later accounts would tell that there were so many reservists, they had had to add on extra carriages at the back of the *express del norte*, and that some of the young volunteers who arrived late had traveled on foot over the cordillera of the Andes – covered in snow at that time of year – to catch the boat at Buenos Aires.

The journey was long. The sea filled Lazare with both dread and amazement. While Robert spent the whole day reading in his cabin and Charles exercised on deck, Lazare smoked cigarettes and listened to the rumors swirling among the recruits. In the morning, they all joined together in rousing military songs and heroic marches, but as the sun went down, they huddled in circles telling horrifying stories of dead birds raining down from the sky at the front, of black fever spawning snails in the stomach, of Germans carving their initials into their prisoners' skin, of the return of diseases not seen since the time of the Baron de Pointis. Once again Lazare thought of France as a dream, and after forty days, when the coast came into view, he realised that the only possibility he had never envisaged was that it really existed.

To disembark, he wore corduroy trousers, thin-soled loafers and a cable-knit jacket handed down from his father. Dressed Chilean-style, he set foot in the port with the naïvety of the adolescent he had been, not the pride of the soldier he was to become. Charles wore a sailor's outfit, a blue-striped shirt and a cotton hat topped with a red pompom. He had styled himself a fine, perfectly symmetrical mustache to adorn his lip like his glorious Gallic ancestors, smoothing the points with a little saliva. Robert had donned a tuxedo shirt, satin trousers and a silver watch on a chain above his waist, which, on the day of his death, was discovered still to be set to Chilean time.

The first thing they noticed as they walked onto the quay was the smell, which was almost identical to that of the port of

Valparaíso. But there was no time to dwell on this, for as soon as they disembarked they were lined up before their company command and handed their uniforms: red trousers, a double-breasted greatcoat, gaiters and a pair of leather boots. They boarded one of the military trucks destined for the battlefields, carrying thousands of immigrants come to tear each other to shreds at the very heart of the continent their fathers had left, never to return. Sitting face-to-face on benches, nobody spoke the French Lazare had read in books, with its flashes of wit and choice turns of phrase; instead, orders were barked unpoetically, insults thrown at an unseen enemy, and on their arrival that night, as Lazare queued in front of the four huge cast-iron casseroles in which the two cooks were reheating a bony stew, all he heard were Breton and Provençal dialects. For a split second, he was tempted to reboard the boat, go back home the way he had come, but he remembered the promise he had made and decided that if there was any patriotic duty that went beyond borders, it was that of fighting to defend the land of your forebears.

For the first few days, Lazare Lonsonier was so busy shoring up trenches, putting in wooden posts and metal grates and laying criss-crossed boards along the ground, that he hadn't time to feel homesick for Chile. He and his brothers spent more than a year putting up barbed wire, sharing out food rations and transporting cases of explosives from one line to the next, coming under fire as they followed the long tracks between artillery batteries. To begin with, to keep their soldierly dignity, they washed sparingly when they found a source of clean water, using a small piece of soap which covered their arms in gray lather. They allowed their beards to grow, out of fashion rather than negligence, so that they too could have the honor of being referred to as *poilus*. But as the months passed, dignity came at a humiliating price. In groups of

11

ten, they set about the degrading exercise of delousing, standing naked in a field with their clothes plunged into boiling water, polishing their rifles with a mixture of sweat and grease before stepping back into their frayed, torn, muddy uniforms, the smell of which would haunt Lazare well into the darkest days of the rise of Nazism.

A rumor went round that anyone who brought back information from the enemy front would be given thirty francs. In the worst of conditions, famished infantrymen soon began to try their luck, climbing over worm-ridden bodies. They lay in the muck like animals, peeking through cracks, peering over the *chevaux-de-frise* in hopes of catching a date, a time, any sign of impending attack. Far from their billets, they sneaked along German lines, trembling with fear and cold in their secret lookouts, sometimes spending entire nights huddled in shell craters. The only one to get his thirty francs was Augustin Latour, a cadet from Manosque. He said he had found a German lying at the foot of a sharp drop, his neck broken by the fall, and had searched his pockets. He had found nothing except some letters written in German, a few paper Deutschmarks and small metal coins with a square hole in the center, but in a secret leather pouch tucked inside the soldier's belt he spotted thirty francs in notes, carefully folded into six, which must have been stolen from the body of a Frenchman. He held them proudly aloft, repeating, "I've got France's money back."

It was around this time that a well was discovered halfway between the two trenches. To his dying day, Lazare Lonsonier never understood how the two enemy lines had come to agree a ceasefire to allow each side to reach it. Around midday, they would all stop firing, and a French soldier would have half an hour to get out of his trench, fill up his heavy buckets of water and carry them back. When the half-hour was up, a German soldier would take his turn to replenish his buckets. Once both fronts were adequately supplied, the guns started up again. They survived in this way in order to carry on killing one another. This black dance was repeated every day with military precision, neither side overrunning their allotted time, strictly respecting the chivalric codes of war, and when they returned from the well, the chosen soldiers said that for the first time in two years of fighting, they had heard distant birdsong, or the whirr of a mill.

Lazare Lonsonier put himself forward. Loaded with four buckets hanging from his forearms, twenty empty flasks across his shoulder and a washing-up basin in his hands, he reached the well after ten minutes of walking, all the while wondering how he would make it back once these same receptacles were filled. Built of old bricks and surrounded by a crumbling wall, the well was as sorry a sight as an aviary empty of birds. Bullet-strewn basins littered the ground around it and a soldier's jacket had been left lying over the edge.

He tied the bucket handle to a rope and lowered it until he heard a splash. He was beginning to pull it back up when a shape suddenly loomed before him like a rock.

Lazare lifted his head. Standing covered in camouflage mud, a German soldier was pointing his gun at him. Terrified, Lazare let go of the rope, dropping the bucket. He straightened up and tried to run, but tripped over a stone and cried out, "*Pucha!*"

He waited for the shot, but none came. He slowly opened his eyes and turned towards the soldier. The soldier stepped forward; Lazare shrank back. The German must have been around the same age as him, but his uniform, boots and helmet all made him look older. He lowered his pistol and asked, "*Eres chileno?*"

The question was whispered in perfect Spanish, a Spanish of fierce condors and *arrayanes*, cormorants and eucalyptus-scented rivers.

"*Sí*," replied Lazare.

The soldier looked relieved.

"*De dónde eres?*" he asked.

"*De Santiago.*"

The German smiled.

"*Yo también. Me llamo Helmut Drichmann.*"

Lazare suddenly recognized the young neighbor from Calle Santo Domingo who had asked him, ten years earlier, where his name came from. News of the war had reached them both at the same time. Both had been drawn across the ocean to defend another country, another flag, but now, standing before this water well, for the space of an instant, they silently returned to drink at the source of their birth.

"*Escúchame*," said the German. "A surprise attack is planned for Friday night. Find a way to be sick and spend the night in the infirmary. It could save your life."

Helmut Drichmann delivered these words in one breath, unplanned and uncalculated. He said them as you would give water to another man, not because you have it, but because you know what thirst is like. The German slowly took off his helmet, and only then could Lazare see him clearly. There was a marble-like beauty to his heavy, matte face, whose patina called to mind the understated charm of old statues. Lazare thought of all the soldiers who had slept in ditches in the hopes of overhearing a conversation, learning where a platoon or machine-gun position was hidden, and the significance of the secret hit home, clear and absurd, like all the great and base events of history.

That day, he faced the first in a long series of dilemmas that would confront generations to come. Should he save himself by hiding out in the infirmary, or protect his fellow soldiers by reporting what he knew to his superiors? Unable to choose, he was in silent turmoil. When he got back to the French lines and his eyes met those of his comrades, he feared they would see him for what he was: both a liar and a traitor.

The conclusion he reached, out of love for Chile, was that he must respect the secret Helmut Drichmann had just told him. He imagined an impossible middle ground between deception and admission. He tried to find a clue, a sign to convince him he had made the right decision, but faced with his weary comrades, he remained hesitant and uncertain. Seeing Charles and Robert lying under filthy blankets on their straw mattresses, he felt such a strong sense of shame that he realized his decision no longer held. He understood that, deep down, true fraternity bound him to another choice. He didn't fully grasp the implications immediately. He didn't suspect for a minute that he had just endured the pain of his first injury, but an hour after his return, he discreetly informed his superior officer of the impending German attack. When he was offered his thirty-franc reward, he refused it.

That Thursday, Lazare's squad attacked at dawn with a hundred and fifty well-armed men and the Germans, taken by surprise in their sleep, were unable to repel the offensive. They threw grenades into straw beds, burned food stores, executed prisoners, released packs of dogs, shot hostages. Over the course of several hours, they committed the same abuses they had condemned among their enemy. Soon the French were the only ones left standing, the defeated soldiers writhing in the mud at their feet. Lazare scoured the steaming plain for the body of Helmut Drichmann. He turned over corpses, deciphered badges, bending over every uniform, his eyes glued to the ground, so absorbed in his task that he failed to notice the shell exploding next to him.

The bomb went off a meter away with devastating force. Many

years later, at the end of his life, departing this world from his house on Santo Domingo, Lazare would remember with terrifying precision the blast that propelled him into a neighboring dugout and smashed his ribs against a rock. The impact tore open his left side and left a hole so deep that his lung was visible through layers of earth and rain. Before losing consciousness, he thought he saw Helmut Drichmann's face peering over him. Then he let himself slip into an otherworldly abyss, and forgot the scene entirely until one day, thirty years later when this same German soldier, laden with gold and mud, came to find him in his living room and accompany him to his death.

Thérèse

The fall did not kill him. Lazare Lonsonier lay unconscious as he waited for a doctor to arrive from the rear trenches and apply antiseptic, and for three nights, only the convulsions of his chest proved he was still alive. He was given injections of camphor oil, morphine and opium to ease the pain, but nothing worked. One rainy Tuesday, he became the first patient to undergo a lobectomy and, unusually, retained hazy memories and vague sensations of a procedure which would become one of the greatest achievements of modern medicine. He was ill for many weeks and finally awoke with a heavy head and puffy eyelids in a hospital that must once have been a traditional Normandy homestead of three floors and four balconies, whose bedrooms still bore the traces of the happy family they had once housed.

The room in which he found himself must have belonged to the children because the window onto the balcony, painted in the colors of exotic birds, did not open. He saw for the first time all the bandages in which he had been wrapped and the white linen dressing on his left shoulder. When he asked about his brothers, he was told Charles had been bayoneted near Arras, having fought passionately until dawn through a night of fierce fighting. Robert had died the next morning, a rifle in one hand and a bottle of wine in the other. He had been charged by a tank, just as the German trench was on the brink of defeat, not far from the very land in which his ancestors had planted their vines. When he heard these two pieces of news, with his sides thickly swaddled, he felt such pain that he began to cough violently and, as he jolted in his bed, knocked his head against the headboard. He fell into another deep, dark coma as if tumbling into a well without a rope or wall to help him out, his body racked with spasms and convulsions, and it was feared he would wake up crazy. Never, in all the years that followed, could Lazare Lonsonier think of the war without reliving the bitter turmoil of those days and, even after he recovered and was granted leave, the lightness that had once graced his heart could never be regained.

During his convalescence, he was given a desk job writing condolence letters to the Spanish-speaking families of fallen soldiers. Sitting at an old typewriter, the first letter he wrote was to his mother. Then, on and on, from one message to the next, he had to tell every desperate sister, every inconsolable wife, every despondent father, the story of the glorious operations in which their son, husband or brother had taken part, finding the right words to underline their courage, daring to place the noblest, most harrowingly poetic last words on their lips. He sent almost a thousand missives, which ended up in a thousand drawers on another continent, sometimes taking six months to arrive, like fragments of memory which mothers stored carefully among *cueca* scarves and copper tablets, a thousand letters which defied moths and oblivion to be read again by the next generation.

Lazare was soon given access to registers of births, deaths and marriages. Being relatively close to the Jura, he thought he would easily be able to pinpoint among the yellowed records of the municipal archive the only man who, to his knowledge, could still remember the history of the family before it had fled France.

He remembered his father talking about an uncle named Michel René, and set about tracking him down. Yet not only were there no Renés, nor Lonsoniers, but he became lost in an incomprehensible jungle of complex family trees and gave up after several weeks of dogged searching, having come to the conclusion that all that remained in these arcane texts were paper corpses and anonymous ghosts. Thus of the four years of war, Lazare Lonsonier spent one in the trenches, two in hospital, and the last in an office in the town hall.

On November 11, 1918, the bells of every church in France pealed to herald the end of the war. In December, when Lazare was sent, along with hundreds of other young Latin Americans, to board a ship heading for Valparaíso, the soul of this wounded country seemed already to have deserted him, and the bucolic countryside he had heard so much about, of châteaux and rows of alders, was now peopled only by the specters of sorry soldiers. From the deck of the ship, he looked out over the landscape and saw distant valleys fertilised by the blood of men killed in combat, green with buried corpses, the lush ground nourished by mounds of dead horses and mass graves.

"This country looks ready to host another war," he thought.

The day Lazare Lonsonier's ship berthed at the port of Valparaíso, his mother was waiting for him on the quay. She had grown old, her face lined with worry, looking paler and more fragile than she had when he left her, with the swollen eyelids of those who have cried many silent tears. She was suddenly reminded of the afternoon when she had waved all three sons off to France and now, seeing only one return, she was barely able to recognize him, and confused his name with those of his two brothers for several months afterwards.

At the age of fifty-two, Delphine had lost the vermilion intensity of her dahlia-like hair. More solitary than ever, she had become unstable, like a wax statuette with a labyrinth of blue veins visible through translucent skin that was rarely exposed to the sun. After receiving the devastating letter informing her of her sons' deaths, she had become obsessive. Ahead of Lazare's return, she had given orders for the walls of her living room to be scrubbed with a soft soap made of oil and brambles, to purify the soul of the house and drive off warlike spirits. She spent many long hours wandering the high plains of senility without complaint, but plagued by unspoken nightmares and muddled hopes, living within the folds of empty time, until one December night when she became convinced that the family woes could be blamed on weapons. Terrified by anything metallic, she took it upon herself to melt down all the saucepans, door hinges and stair balustrades and turn them into sparkling jewelry, thereby transforming all that reminded her of death into the cast metal of life. Which is why, when Lazare returned from the war covered in decorations, military stripes and medals depicting a woman surrounded by laurels in bas-relief, she fused them with gold in a crucible, repeating over and over again that no military honor and no war pension could ever replace her children, and made them into rings which remained on her fingers until her final hour.

Not wishing to feel cut off from France, Lazare read all the press that reached Santiago. He flicked through newspapers and bought periodicals, lapping up every story. He convinced himself that by sacrificing his youth, he had given more to France than all the exiles of the previous century had done through the prestige of their wines. The Great War had left Chile fractured. Its farming operations, run-down factories and depleted reserves could no longer be relied upon. It became harder to import goods, and injections of foreign capital had decreased. The French began setting up sections of the Union des Poilus, Pompe France firefighter companies and veterans' associations in almost every town. They spoke of Verdun and the Chemin des Dames, told escape stories, compared medals, quoted Clemenceau by his nickname "Le Tigre." The *latifundistas* of yesterday marked their calling cards with the number of estates they owned. Today, they were printed with their war wounds.

Yet this feeling of patriotic power could not blot out the images of Lazare's lost years. His heart was like the vine in his garden, planted twenty-four years earlier on the day of his birth, which had taken on a dull color and off-putting smell, was almost devoid of foliage and no longer produced grapes. Lazare began once more to have visions of apocalypse and bouts of fever and coughing which left him sweating under bloodstained sheets. His head was filled with the sounds of explosions and the clash of sabers, the thud of rifle butts and the whoosh of rockets soaring up in the sky. Visions of his lung operation often came back to him. In lyrical bursts of delirium, he would tell the story in hideous, shocking detail, recounting the smell of turps and the crumbling walls of the infirmary, and explaining that at the end, when they had sewn him up and shown him the half-lung they had amputated, he thought they were presenting him with a piece of his own heart.

French doctors were called – the only "true" doctors in the land, according to his father. One by one a succession of scientists and pharmacists appeared at his bedside, trained by the Pasteur school, disciples of Augustin Cabanès, or literature fans who took themselves for Balzac's Dr. Horace Bianchon. Sitting in a circle in the living room drinking hot coffee, they debated among themselves for hours, proposing complex remedies, some wishing to send him for a cure at an avant-garde health center in Limache, others calling for the Coué method, popular at the time. Lazare accepted every treatment, followed the doctors' instructions to the letter, and raised no objection to any regime. But the tablets simply gave him migraines, throbbing temples, an inflamed brow and a skewed right eye, and he felt as if his brain were exploding inside his head like a hundred pieces of shrapnel tearing across a battlefield. The cough persisted; his temperature remained high. Everyone, even his closest family, was surprised to see him still alive. He would wake up in tears, his chest red with fear, the wound over his lung drained of blood. Defeated, he would then fall back on his sheets, his muscles weak, his skin pale, with the horrifying sensation that Helmut Drichmann was staring at him from the other side of the bed, leaky bucket in hand.

Lonsonier senior, who was now sixty-four years of age and beginning to add new varieties to his hectares of vineyards, was so concerned for his son's health that he was forced to concede medical progress had been quietly defeated.

"It's not a doctor you need, it's a *machi*," he declared.

In those days, a famous Mapuche healer or *machi* by the name of Aukan practiced in Santiago, captivating the masses as much as he repelled the scientists. This strange fellow, who was destined to play an essential role in the family's history, claimed to have been born in Tierra del Fuego from an unbroken line of sorcerers and witch doctors. He had crossed the Araucanía on foot, fleeing the missionaries and Jesuit monks who were founding communities there, making a living by devoting himself to the teachings of supernatural medicine, filling the gap where natural medicine had failed. He had a faintly mischievous smile, bracelets around his wrists and a ring on his index finger found inside the belly of a fish. Long black hair tied with an indigenous barrette fell down his back, which was broad as an oak. Always dressed in a poncho which left one shoulder exposed, he wore a thick silver belt adorned with bunches of cascabel chillies, and vicuña-skin trousers whose crease brushed the tops of his shoes. When he smiled, his teeth had a bluish gleam, and when he talked, strange words with mystical inflections and an accent that was hard to place seemed to come not from another country but another time – a language so singular it was impossible to say whether it already existed, or if he was making it up on the spot.

When Aukan crossed the living room and saw the young man consumed by fever, delirium and wheezing coughs, he gathered up the collection of medicines which had accumulated on the table, threw them out of the window, drew the curtains and announced with theatrical solemnity: "The remedy is more dangerous than the disease itself."

Aukan relied only on oral medicines, prophetic dreams and alchemists' almanacs. Having carefully studied and run his finger around the scar on Lazare's torso, he finally began his defense of secret sciences and dialogues with the dead. He gathered the whole family in the room to explain what he knew about lungs, and succeeded in persuading Lazare of the irrefutable benefits of shamanistic rituals for his recovery.

"Everything lies in the past," he said. "The first thing you must do is reconnect with your *pillanes*. The souls of your ancestors."

Lazare mumbled something about a certain Michel René, a French uncle he had been told about, but Aukan seemed unconvinced as he moved his cascabels aside, piled herbs into a mortar with the blood of a black hen which had known no cockerel, and began pounding them into a poultice. Accompanying his movements with incantations, he coated Lazare's wound with a sticky greenish paste which he mixed with a lock of hair. From that morning, he made Lazare wear an old goatskin, a reddish jacket with the hair on the inside and worn-out elbows, which stank of decomposing rodents, and forbade him to touch his side. If Lazare was willing to entertain this curious treatment, it was because he had long since realized the vanity of putting up a fight against death and decided, as the end drew near, that he might as well rot from the inside. The poultice was left on his scar for a week and, after ten days, a smell of wilted flowers began to emanate from the wound, filling the air with a repulsive intestinal stench until a dry, brown scab formed like a roll of cinnamon. The smell was so fetid that no one dared visit him in his house on Santo Domingo, and a rumor went round the neighborhood that Lazare had come back from the Marne with scorpions in his belly.

It was Delphine who, infuriated by the foul odor, burst into his room one day and declared: "It's not a witch doctor you need, but a wife."

In late November, when the days were growing finer and longer, the Lonsonier family began taking picnics to the fields of Pirque, an hour outside the capital. The countryside was perfectly silent but for the piercing cries of raptors circling high in the sky. One Sunday, Lazare split off from the group and began walking through the meadow to breathe in the smells of haymaking. With the old goatskin over his shoulders, he was wandering aimlessly through the long grass when in the distance he suddenly saw a group of merchants selling spices and jewelry from a circle of carts.

They were young men with olive skin, strong, skillful hands and eyes shaped like arrow tips, selling women's jewelry from the Araucanía. They laid out necklaces made in the silver mines and basketwork from Nacimiento, and with heavily tattooed arms showed off displays of feathers and rugs, copper bracelets and painted gourds. An old man opened a cage for him in which enormous white lizards were sleeping motionless on piles of leaves, their bellies filled with wasps.

"What do you want to buy?" he asked.

"I want to buy a journey," Lazare replied.

Inured to the unpredictable folly of the white man, the Mapuche did not bat an eyelid and replied that if he had the means to pay them for a month, they would allow him to join their caravan. Lazare seized the offer as enthusiastically as he had joined the army. Not wishing his mother to worry, he scribbled a message on a scrap of paper and had it taken back to the picnickers by one of the children. Half an hour later, when Delphine saw the long-haired, bare-legged mixed-race boy approaching with a coarse woollen blanket over his shoulders, she knew immediately that her son had gone to tend the secret wounds the Marne had inflicted on him. With the family gathered around her, she read aloud the words written in a decisive hand.

I have left with the future.

Lazare's second and last journey towards Cajón del Maipo took twenty-one days. He rode through barren landscapes, towards communities who bred wild cats and hunted guanacos on foot. He spent entire days climbing peaks and descending slopes where the hooves of wild beasts gleamed on the rocks, crossing alfalfa fields where dusk bloomed as pink as a puma's gums. Every summit carried a giant cross unfelled by wind or storm. For a time he dealt in chinchilla and viscacha furs, surviving off corn soup with avocado oil. He stayed in the valleys where he met *huasos*, cattle herders who rode bareback, chewing grass and rolling coca leaves under their tongues as they sold their wares from town to town. The indigenous people reeled off the names of insects, speaking of them like people they knew, and told him about plains where the sheep's wool was harder than iron and the women could turn into narwhals.

The pure air, the journey far from anywhere and the endless discoveries of the land all helped to heal his wounded lung. The succession of *meseta* plateaus – open, covered in thorns or scattered with purple basalt – proved greater remedies than any of Aukan's poultices. Lazare felt so well that after two weeks he decided to leave the group and head back up towards the cordillera, as the Castilian conquistadors had aimed to. In mid-December, he put up his tent and stopped for a few days in the fruit-filled orchard of a former *fundo* with the remains of a kitchen garden and irrigation channel dug by Belgian settlers, deep in a valley on the banks of the Río Clarillo.

Picking apples in a meadow with the goatskin around his neck one Tuesday, he found himself shoved to the ground as two powerful talons dug into the skin between his shoulder blades. Lazare struggled furiously and the bird, surprised to be facing resistance, backed off, flapping its wings. Lazare turned round to see the magnificent gray creature hanging in the air a meter away from him. It was an Andean black-chested buzzard-eagle which, confused by the goatskin, had swooped down on him as if tracking a rodent. Before he had a chance to react, he heard a voice in Spanish.

"Sorry about that. She took you for a fox. You're not hurt, are you?"

The terror of the trenches had left him with rather brusque manners. He replied mechanically in French, as if to reassure a fellow soldier: "*Ça va!*"

He made an about-turn and studied the person who had spoken. He was stunned to discover that the owner of this bird of prey was not a rugged countryman reeking of caravan trips over high plains, but a young, elegant, gentle woman with a slender figure who had suddenly appeared before him, dressed in men's clothes. She had white, perfectly straight teeth, and a cream felt hat which cast a delicate shadow down to her lips.

"*Eres francés?*" she asked.

Lazare blushed. He thought his face would explode from the blood rushing to his cheeks, and the burning sensation sent him redder still.

"*Sí.*"

The woman put on her leather glove and the bird landed on her fist.

"My family is French," she said.

Lazare was amazed to find that the young woman's hands were not calloused or thickened by the wearing of leather gloves, but seemed to have been crafted from the finest silver. With her freckles, deep-red hair and dark eyes in which sadness and shyness were combined, she had something of a young Occitanian. She had a little nose, a smooth brow and a pointy chin, which reminded him of the laurel-covered profile of the woman on the medals of those who died for France. They walked together across the plain, whose scents were even more heady in the heat of the day. Lazare mentioned the war.

"*Cuál guerra?*" she asked.

Lazare made no reply. The more they spoke, the more he could see that she was a generous, welcoming person who tried her best to make others happy, and he understood what an unexpected gift a caravan of indigenous travelers had accidentally brought him. He could not remember feeling so awkward, so ashamed of his big hands, fragile health and gangling arms since he had looked at himself in the mirror before he went to war. The next day, he found her standing on a rose-covered hillock, feeding the bird from her hand. For a moment he was disappointed not to glimpse the feeling he thought he had seen in her eyes the previous day. But over the next four days, as they continued to walk together often, Lazare began searching for the fault line through which he might find a way to her heart.

When he learned she was called Thérèse Lamarthe, Lazare –

who had been a great reader in his youth – recognized the name of a tragic French character. Thérèse must have been around eighteen, with a friendly femininity and sure step inherited from her distant ancestors. She tied her hair in a chignon on top of her head and gave off the fresh scent of raptor and leather with every move she made. In those days, women left their houses enshrouded in black lace mantles, loose hooded cloaks which covered their shoulders and hid their hips beneath their wide folds. Yet Thérèse wore a French hat and elegant, frivolous trinkets, in contrast with the practicality of her trade.

Lazare knew nothing about women, still less the ways of seduction. So, more through ignorance than gallantry, he courted her in an old-fashioned, rather clumsy way, so that in the end it was Thérèse who took him firmly by the hand one evening, as they sat side by side on the roots of a poplar, and her determination revived his soldierly courage. She would always remember how, looking into his pink-lidded eyes, she thought she saw the haze of an untimely end.

"This man will die young," she thought.

Not a month had passed since the picnic in Pirque when Lazare returned to Santo Domingo strong and rejuvenated, speaking a Spanish peppered with Mapuche words, as Thérèse traveled nomad-like on the cart behind him, a ring made from a reed wrapped around her finger. At the sight of her son and future daughter-in-law, Delphine was flushed with emotion, and when she rushed to pass on news of the engagement to old Lonsonier in his rocking chair, he was bursting with admiration.

"My boy!" he exclaimed. "He went and found himself a Frenchwoman among the Indians."

The marriage took place in the second week of December. Thérèse was dressed in a blue satin dress with *petit point* stitching and a long tulle train held by two young girls. All the French families in Santiago and the surrounding towns were invited to the bishop's blessing at the cathedral, with guests arriving from the flanks of the cordillera carrying cases of their finest wine, big white vases and wreaths of cascading flowers. Two sheep were sacrificed and spit-roasted in the garden to be served on plates painted in the style of Bonnard, and the evening ended in the living room on Santo Domingo, where every faded cushion had been embroidered with the interlacing initials of husband and wife.

Around midnight, Thérèse went up to the bedroom. When Lazare came to join her, there was steam in the air, as if someone had run a bath. He lit a match and a fragile flame carved a circle of light from the gloom. It was then he saw Thérèse lying naked in the middle of the bed, radiating youth and arrogant beauty. He had never guessed that a woman's body could hold such contours, peaks, ravines and fault lines. It was as if his wife had been hiding her virginity away, guarding it from prying eyes like a timid falcon, and it seemed to Lazare she had been saving it for his embraces. When he touched her body, her skin was as soft as peach fuzz, after hours of sponging with amber molasses, and smelled of honey. But when he brought his face closer to hers, he was struck by a strong scent of lemon which suddenly brought the battlefields and their legacy vividly back to him.

Lazare moved away from her, his body closing like a fist. All at once his muscles tensed, his mouth crumpled and his head spun. Muttering faint words of apology, he stood up from the bed and crossed the room, filled with shame, revealing to his wife the imperfections of both his body and heart.

She saw then that her husband bore a silent wound which could at any time be reopened by a rash move, unexpected scent or misspoken word. She was beginning to get to know the man behind the awkward silences filled with secret hurts. Though she had not lived through the anguish and agony of the war, she felt the same sense of sacrifice and veneration that occupied his mind could also inhabit her own.

To calm him down, she led him to the bath, sprinkling cornflowers and coriander over the surface of the water. He sat still as she sponged him and rubbed coconut oil into the wound on his chest. Working carefully and meticulously, she made his rough skin smooth again, massaged his knotted muscles and then slowly, innocently, plunged her hand between his legs, and with skill and application, gave him back a vigor he had thought lost. Only then did she slide into the water with him like an aquatic plant, resting her head on his chest and drawing him towards her as she lay still, filled with devotion, embracing the prospect of the thousand nights, heartaches and epiphanies to come.

The water which once had separated him from Helmut Drichmann now joined him to the woman with whom he was discovering love for the first time. Lazare felt his heart swell with brave, avid, uncontrollable desire and, as he acted upon it, the claw-foot bath shook so enthusiastically that the light bulb hanging in the entrance hall below began to flicker. For the next month, he blushed as his neighbors greeted him with newfound respect. Lazare would never forget the night his wife had brought back the scent of citrus, of gloom, sweat and piled-up bodies, and how they had lain entwined in the cast-iron tub which had belonged to the first Lonsonier, and was large enough to welcome the generation to come.

El Maestro

In 1887, a young trumpet player from Sète named Étienne Lamarthe left the village brass band and took his music to the other side of the world, carrying thirty-three wind instruments in cypress wood trunks sealed shut with silver nails. The young man with pale skin and dark hair, who spoke not a word of Spanish, disembarked at Valparaíso with fourteen flutes, eight saxophones, six clarinets, four trumpets and an enormous tuba in a metal case so heavy it was suspected of harboring a stowaway. Over the next three days, he traveled nine leagues in a cart drawn by a blind mule, taking his orchestra across the plains through stifling heat, watching over his instruments with a mother's loving care and harmonious incantations until he reached Limache, a village in the province of Marga Marga where tomatoes and orchids grew.

He moved into a house with an inner courtyard and concrete floors zebra-striped like pages of sheet music. The very next day he started recruiting volunteers to join his music theory lessons and start a little band. He nailed a sign under his porch for all to see, on which he had written "Music School" in broken Spanish. Then he opened his door – never to close it again for the next sixty-seven years – announcing his arrival to all the poetic souls of Limache.

The bare, unfurnished living room had scarcely been dusted

down before it was transformed into a school filled with young bakers learning to blow into flutes and farmers discovering how to tune a clarinet, and young washerwomen patiently playing scales amid the silence of the pine trees. When a piano was sent for from Santiago, it arrived missing its feet and two black keys, battered at the edges, having been carried on a cart loaded with crates of watermelons, and was tuned by a cobbler using bootlaces. A broken harp was acquired along with some sickly looking violins, worn and white at the handles, but which Étienne Lamarthe restored with such passion and devotion that when he died, they came to be considered sacred relics.

His lessons were soon regularly attended and there were plenty of musicians at every rehearsal. The village police tolerated the noise after dark; never had there been such melodious nights, when trumpets muffled by widows' headscarves sounded until dawn. Within three months the new, dedicated artistes of this remote hamlet were ready to perform their humble repertoire in front of the village hall, and thus, before an audience of rivers and hills, the first baroque music concert was held in Limache.

The concert was such a success that Étienne Lamarthe, soon nicknamed *El Maestro*, quickly became the most respected man in the region. With his head as full of ideas as his house was of amateur musicians, he had more instruments sent from Lima and São Paulo and founded a symphonic orchestra, devising his own simplified arrangements of Italian operas for musicians who could scarcely have placed Rome on a map. He offered classical singing lessons in his kitchen and, as the new century dawned in 1900, his name was mentioned as far away as the capital. He put on a performance of Bellini's *Norma* here in the depths of the countryside in front of the regional government offices, setting up a stage made of twenty planks and eight wine barrels with a backdrop built by the local gravedigger. A bust of Bellini was made from Chuquicamata copper to commemorate the occasion, and it stood proud and heavy, facing the music school, for the next sixty years, until it was buried alongside El Maestro himself.

Four years after his arrival in Chile, Étienne Lamarthe had become the most eligible bachelor in the region. He married Michèle Moulin, the daughter of a rich French shoemaking family. They had two daughters: Danièle and Thérèse. The girls grew up surrounded by operas and symphonies, learned music theory before they learned Spanish, and their first words were musical notes. Danièle learned the saxophone, while Thérèse, who showed little aptitude for woodwind, developed such a beautiful voice that at eight years old she was able to sing Verdi and Puccini arias without music, becoming renowned for the innocent clarity of her voice.

But one late November day, a whooping cough epidemic struck the village. Despite her solid constitution, Thérèse was soon suffering from a painful cough and the village doctors sent her up to the flanks of the cordillera, where the clean mountain air would do her good. Far away from harmonies and concerts, cut off from the grandeur of Verdi and Bellini operas, Thérèse discovered the silence of birds, a silence filled with coos and squawks, stepping into a sacred world in which another pure song reigned supreme.

At the age of sixteen, she moved permanently to a hacienda to study ornithology. She rented a room in the village of Melocotón, perched high in the Río Clarillo national park, which was linked to the rest of the country only by dangerous paths and mule tracks. One day, she joined a roped expedition along the ridge of the cordillera, climbing snowless summits spiked with vertical needles where the sun had melted the ice palaces some months earlier. Their guide was telling them about the plant life at 4,000-meter altitudes, when suddenly his attention was caught by a sound at the edge of a rock face. He motioned to the group to crouch down behind a clump of vegetation. They edged forward, practically crawling along the ground, towards a low rock wall protecting walkers from the precipice beyond. As Thérèse peered through the foliage above the rocks, she saw it.

A giant condor, alone on the mountain, immense against the abyss, with a coat of metallic feathers and a bare head emerging from a ring of white. A ridge of hard yellow and mauve skin ran between its eyes, criss-crossed with veins and slightly twisted at the tip like the bark of an oak tree. The group stood completely still, holding their breath, watching the dark tranquility of this creature walking around its nest like a monster guarding its lair. The condor straightened up and surveyed the valley with its disdainful, perfect gaze. Only then did it clack its tongue and open its wings, covering a span of three and a half meters in a single movement. It threw its beak back, puffed out its chest and sent a hollow sound out from its belly to the open expanse below. It sounded at first like a clash of stone, a repeated lament, a kind of broken sneeze, and then it lengthened into a wild, sharp blast, like a tree being uprooted and the echo traveling for miles around. It wasn't a cry but a sublimely ugly purr, a strange kind of music, and when the sound had reached its peak, it faded to a brief, piercing whistle, finally giving way to an imperious calm.

Thérèse was more enthralled by this than anything else she saw until ten years later, when she gave birth to a little girl in a bronze aviary. She saw, perhaps, a kind of warning in the sublime and ignoble discovery that the animal held in the depths of its throat all that opera tried to express through her. Only certain steep-sided valleys, certain mountains, certain geological peculiarities could measure up to the greatest arias. This pure, unwily, naïve girl, raised to sing before the world, felt herself undergoing a transformation whose significance she could not yet grasp.

At the age of eighteen, she moved on from studying birds to training raptors. In those days, falconry was practiced only by a few rare enthusiasts who trained harriers to hunt under cloudless skies on dry, game-filled plains, in a strictly masculine environment. She found it hard to carve out a place for herself among this nest of men with talon-like hands, who saw omens in every flight and whose hours spent watching their falcons hunting had made them more resistant to friendship. Thérèse entered a world in which birds were no longer a symbol of poetic inspiration, of freedom and the promise of escape, but a hook-nosed mob of dark myth, whose cries were like croaking toads and whose claws could tear through lead.

These were difficult times for Thérèse, of friction within the group and unfair treatment due to her sex. Her naturally delicate features still showed the same yearning as ever, but hunting had triggered an inner revolt which had changed the expression on her face. She was twenty when she gained her falconry license. She had managed to tame an Andean black-chested buzzard-eagle with pale feathers and a slate-flecked breast, whose eyes could pick out a tiny coin from a hundred-meter distance. She named the bird Niobe for its stone color. She carried it artfully on her wrist, with a cord tied around its feet, as though her arm were a hazel branch. She weighed it every day before each training session, noting down the quantity of food given, the type of exercise undertaken and how quickly it responded to being called back mid-flight. Once the bird could be lured with confidence and took food from her fist, she began walking it through the undergrowth and across wind-battered plateaux, over hectares of exposed land crossed only by solitary shepherds and peregrines.

Within a month, the buzzard-eagle could hunt. Glimpsing its quarry in the distance, it would tense its muscles like a leopard preparing to pounce, extending its neck as it stared at the plain, digging its talons into the leather and leaping up into the air. It became used to flying further afield, skirting the dry lands covered in laurels and bush flowers where travelers sometimes pitched their tents.

One day when the wind carried a distant whiff of carrion, the buzzard-eagle followed its instinct towards the stench of an elusive carcass. Flying high in the sky, it eventually spotted a fox's fur among the grass and struck, attacking from behind with lightning speed, its talons spread out in front of it, focusing all its energy in one incredible swoop – and went crashing into a goatskin coat.

The bird retreated, frightened by a mass much larger than itself. Lazare Lonsonier let out a cry. Man and bird both leapt back in surprise. Thérèse ran straight towards them.

"Sorry about that," she exclaimed. "She took you for a fox."

They saw each other again over the days that followed, and in their thirty years of marriage, whenever Lazare took a bath with Thérèse, he thanked God for the day Aukan had laid a goatskin over his shoulders. After their wedding night, Thérèse fell pregnant. Her face took on the color of a sprig of chamomile. She ate only ruby-colored duracine cherries and *choclo* corn soup, and began rubbing aloe vera gel over her belly to prevent stretch marks. So strong and healthy was she that she made it through the first ten weeks without a hint of nausea. She covered her breasts in sugar cane juice to prevent cracking. To improve the quality of her milk, she ate carefully and intoned magical incantations to ward off the evil eye. Since her marriage she had tended to her husband, shaving his beard and filling his bath with warm water to soothe his lung, and now it fell to him to run her baths, powder her neck and cut her toenails with silver scissors.

Delphine and old Lonsonier could see that the couple needed space. Quietly, mysteriously, they slipped out of the house on Santo Domingo and went to live in Santa Carolina. Even Lazare failed to notice that his mother had sunk into a parallel universe, crushed by the terrible sadness of the death of two sons, and it was only when he realized, too late, that he would never see her again that he came to regard his parents' departure as a defining moment in his life.

Just before dusk one afternoon in June, as her inner turmoil began to rage, Delphine left her room in Santa Carolina for her daily walk. She put on a wide-brimmed hat and all the rings she had made from melted-down medals and headed towards a lake where leafless willow branches bent over the water. She was seen setting off for the irrigation lagoon, leaving all the windows and the front door open. She didn't stop at the water's edge but kept walking at the same pace, letting the water wash over her until it covered her completely, as if trying to reach the middle of the lagoon. They say she carried on walking as far as she could breathe, gently rocked by the flow of the underwater meadow, surrounded by dancing pondweed, and two golden fish swam inside her lungs. After a few minutes, her body absorbed half the lake like a manatee, so that she never floated up to the surface. It took three divers to pull her from the slimy waters which had already begun to devour her.

Her tomb was erected on the edge of the forest, on a stone platform covered in begonias and the leaves of cherry trees, sixty-six centimeters deep. Delphine was laid out in an olive-wood coffin with a metal plaque bearing her name. But in the darkness under the earth, a muddy oil oozed out from the pores of her drenched body, thick with the scent of wet grass, swimming with aquatic plants and fish scales. In two days, the tomb was inundated. There was so much sludge coming up from the ground that by the end of the week, the stone was no longer visible, and they had to siphon off forty liters with a hosepipe that became blocked by a bronze ring.

Old Lonsonier went into mourning and never remarried. He retreated from the world, avoiding social norms and niceties, and, on the second Wednesday in July, decided to heal his soul by sending all his wife's belongings to the house on Santo Domingo. Thus news of Delphine's death reached the capital at the same time as the chests and trunks piled up in the entrance hall. The household had not seen so many parcels arrive since the days of the culinary experiments. Over the next nine months, the rooms were filled with baggage, boxes with dragon-shaped handles and toilet articles from another era, with ceramic containers and camel hairbrushes, silk lace and plum-colored veils. Elegant packages arrived pell-mell, barely opened, unharmed by time or moths. Thérèse, by now several months pregnant, oversaw and directed operations from her rattan chair, her hands crossed over the curve of her belly, around which she wore a fake pearl belt. Among all the boxes, one was placed up high with religious care and attention. Many years later, Lazare would remember the first bird arriving in the house that winter inside a Scots pine crate, surrounded by a strong odor of wild garlic.

The cage was yellow, protected by camphor and artificial feathers, with two perches, one of which swung. The cage was so heavy it took two grown men to lift it. It was opened carefully and Thérèse found a sublime creature from the forests of northern France and Belgium inside. It had most likely been captured in

Flanders, at the bottom of Mont Noir near Bailleul, among snow-capped firs and godforsaken belfries.

"Owls bring good luck," she said.

Its plumage was the purple of the magi's robes, but with a russet-colored breast, golden eyes and a short, pointy beak. It had a morose look about it, like a Dutch painter. Thérèse immediately set to caring for it with methodical tenderness, soon aided by Lazare who appraised in jealous silence the animal who had stolen his wife's attention. To begin with, Thérèse wanted to feed the bird in the cage in which it had arrived rather than risk moving and unsettling it. She put music on, as she had read to do, and bought Belgian records to help it feel at home. She cooed over the bird, put special supplements in its feed and forbade it to ever be left alone. The neighbors began talking about it as if it were an exile of the war, saying that since all the forests in France were ablaze, even the birds were jumping on ships. They believed the creature had been conjured from Flemish witchcraft or had flown out of a Scandinavian fairy tale, carrying illnesses dangerous to newborns, but the owl was as unflappable, stubborn and deaf to their talk as a member of the family, adapting to its new home with ease. It grew bigger, had longer feathers, put on weight, and might have come to resemble an eagle had the dictatorship not, years later, put a bullet between its eyes.

Encouraged by the owl's successful acclimatization, Thérèse set about compiling a detailed list of other species that might one day come to live with her. She made occasional visits to the natural history museum, returning home thrilled by what she had read about the diet of the green woodpecker, the mustaches of the bearded tit, the jealousy of lovebirds and the rarity of the bee-eater. As her belly grew bigger, she imported more and more birds, smuggled through customs one by one to join the Lonsonier brood. Sometimes the boxes arrived with speckled, greenish eggs laid during the crossing hidden under tufts of hay, which the servants tried to incubate with warmed sheets, running about in search of places to put them. The rooms of the house were soon filled with cages eroded by the salt of the ocean, battered by a dizzying whirlwind of blackbirds and garganey ducks, melodious linnets and collared crows, skylarks and gray herons fluttering this way and that, drunk on freedom.

Within a month, the birds had outnumbered the human inhabitants of Santo Domingo, and the stifling smell of their droppings hung in the air. They lined up along chipped coat hooks like strings of black notes, sat on ledges that had been installed a few centimeters below the ceiling, chattering like schoolkids, ruffling their feathers and chirruping like castanets. Two siskins in skullcap and bib, which had come bundled together, swooped over the staircases as one, and a mynah bird, which looked like an Italian Madonna, sang among the books in the library. A cuckoo had started dropping its petrol-tinged quills into the nests of other birds. Java sparrow couples built their homes among the folded silks in the wardrobes, from which baby birds could be heard chirping, while stocky little society finches with chevroned white bellies pecked at the still-life paintings, mistaking them for plantain flowers. In every corner, in bathroom and kitchen, there were endless bowls of sunflower seeds, peanuts and ground walnuts, but also ants' eggs and wax worms which Thérèse laid out in neat lines and Lazare swept up in exasperation. They bought a cockerel, as a symbol of France, and even saved a magpie which had walked over smoldering embers and set its own nest ablaze.

It wasn't long before Lazare lost patience. Returning home one day, he took in the extraordinary number of birds, the dropping-smeared windows and ruined rugs, and decided enough was enough.

"If we're all going to live here together, we need our own space."

He decided to build an aviary. He made short trips out of town and returned laden with all kinds of building materials. Wearing big straw-stuffed clogs and an old camlet coat, he cut wood, fixed beams, unfurled mesh panels, slotted in metal fittings, put on a roof and screwed in brackets.

By the time the month was out, an aviary stood in the middle of the garden. It looked like a small pergola, with iron bars and a single door with a bolt in the shape of a salamander. A bronze dome kept the wind out but let the light in, and in the middle was a marble drinking bowl fed by an underground spring. To Lazare, the sound of running water was an almost ostentatious symbol of wealth; he allowed himself the luxury of letting it flow freely simply for the pleasure of hearing the noise it made. Inside the four-meter structure, with a concrete base to keep stone martens out, he set up wicker cages for the turtle doves and little houses for the goldfinches and hung up a dozen cuttlefish bones on which the canaries could sharpen their beaks.

Thérèse organized the exodus. Over the course of a week, she arranged for almost fifty birds of twenty-five different species to be moved. She went regularly to and fro, giving instructions on how the birds' new home should be laid out and checking their food. Holding a book in her hand, she set out sticks made from egg and orange, rediscovering the rural skills of her youth in Río Clarillo. One clear afternoon two days later, as she was filling up the nest boxes, she felt such a sharp pain in her belly that she was forced to sit down in the middle of the aviary. The child was making ferocious movements in her womb, thrashing around deep inside her, but her hard work on the aviary, house and kitchen garden proved sound physical preparation. She closed the door of the cage, lifted the hem of her dress and, as the Java sparrows looked on blankly, readied herself to give birth on the bark-covered floor.

In the hours of screams, deep breaths and contractions that followed, all the local midwives and every child in the neighborhood came running; rarely has a woman given birth in front of so many as Thérèse Lonsonier. Huddled on the floor, she fought against the invisible angel tearing incandescently through her, looking into the strange and shapeless eyes of the sparrows and canaries for guidance. The widening rent between her legs, the drenched and fetid head beginning to appear was both her hard-gained offering to the world and the aviary staking its baptismal claim. A little ball covered in blood and feathers emerged from Thérèse's belly and rolled on its head like an egg amid the chaotic concert of squawks, hoots and cries. Its tiny face, covered in fluff like a vulture, gazed up at the bronze dome from where Thérèse's owl stared down in majestic silence. The little girl curled herself up in the crook of her mother's arm as if snuggling down in her nest, and at that moment something melted in Thérèse's heart, overwhelming her with tenderness. Stunned by the sudden blessing she had received, she lifted the child in her arms, and the birth marked such a profound shift in her that everything thereafter could be divided into the "before" and "after" of that day.

And so Margot was born at eight in the evening on a Saturday feast day. Having first opened her eyes to the sight of fifty birds perched around her, she could never get to sleep anywhere but the aviary. Thérèse had to creep in at dusk, sit on a stool in the middle of the cage and wait for Margot to close her eyes as night fell and swarms of dragonflies and yellow moths closed in around them. Santiago had lost its village feel by then. Gone were the dark mantilla-clad figures, women in wide-brimmed hats, and plaster garlands on the facades of buildings. Now the city was a cosmopolitan capital crisscrossed by tramlines, cables and wide avenues. Tower blocks began to spring up and the suburbs, built on what had once been farmland, now ringed the city like the bark of a tree. Rich families moved into the neighborhoods of La Moneda and Augustinas and took walks around the Plaza de Armas, which had been laid out with winding paths, ponds and bandstands. Everywhere was prosperity, moneymaking, social climbing. La Casa Francesa on Calle Estado, with its huge Parisian sign, added a third shop floor and the Lumière cinema opened opposite the Union Central building.

Every Sunday, Thérèse would take her daughter for a walk through Cerro Santa Lucia. As Margot grew older, it became clear she did not enjoy the company of other children. She didn't run around the garden in an unbuttoned romper suit, drink water off the reeds in the Mapocho or play hide-and-seek among spiky shrubs and wild grasses. Her usual mood was flat, impenetrable, as if she were locked inside an invisible fortress. She showed no interest or curiosity in anything. Buttoned up to the neck in blue lace-collared dresses, she was pale and quiet, displaying no inclination for childhood games. A friendless dreamer, she could go entire days without saying a word. Nothing about her suggested she would one day become a pugnacious, wildly ambitious, stunningly successful woman who would hold people in her thrall.

She had inherited from the Lonsoniers her Jurassian blood, her autumn-colored eyes and dignified demeanor. She embodied the proud silence of the people of the interior. From the Lamarthes, she had got the Mediterranean tendency for sudden minor rebellions at the most unexpected times. The combination of traits meant she could occasionally be overcome with bursts of cheerfulness, brief pleasures, intense moments of joy, but they disappeared as quickly as they had arrived, like ripples on the surface of a pond. Her mother was perhaps the only one to understand that her daughter's tendency for distant daydreaming was not the cold temperament people mistook it for. So it was Thérèse who called for Aukan, who had gained the trust of the Lonsonier family when he had tried to heal Lazare. He came gamboling in, looking so light-footed, youthful and fresh, so sweet-scented and childlike, that Lazare remarked that time seemed to be very kind to witch doctors.

"I'm not a witch doctor," he objected. "I'm a *psychologiste*."

He pronounced this word in French, because it sounded like *artiste*. He was wearing a vicuña skin with a woollen cape which fell over his shoulders. All he carried with him was a small leather knapsack filled with dinosaur bones. He explained that these were the remains of fifteen-ton herbivores twelve meters high which had lived seventy million years ago, discovered during his digs in southern Patagonia.

"These bones are worth more than diamonds," he said proudly.

While he waited to find the right market to sell them, convinced meanwhile that dealers on the archaeological black market were trying to find them, he deemed the house on Santo Domingo a suitable hiding place for them. This was how prehistoric fossils came to be stored in a biscuit tin on a kitchen shelf, a young nurse confusing them with chicken feet more than forty years later.

With his mind put at ease, Aukan took a seat opposite Margot, who was ensconced in a wicker chair sucking her thumb and watching him with big, vacant eyes. Thérèse asked if he had children, to which he replied: "I've a hundred."

Along with the dinosaur pieces in his pocket, he had brought a treasure meant for Margot alone. In hazy light, to the clinking sound of his bracelets, Aukan gave a speech he appeared to have learned by heart. It was a story of travels through snow-capped peaks and pampas grasslands, of mystical paths and winter forests where *ibadou*-consuming Mapuche lived. He explained that when the indigenous people chewed the *ibadou* plant, they were able to lift themselves four meters off the ground.

"When I ran my stick beneath their feet or above their heads to see if there was some ruse at work, I realized they really were levitating."

Margot shifted in her seat.

"Levitating?" she repeated, looking questioningly at her mother.

"*Machi* stories," Thérèse explained with a dismissive wave of the hand.

Aukan took from his bag a small white tuber, hard and dry like a fern root, which he rubbed between his hands.

"*Ibadou* is much more than that."

He put his palms together, pushed his nose between them and inhaled deeply. His eyes rolled back and his cheeks turned pale.

"Will you lend me your ring?" he asked Thérèse.

Aukan took it. Frowning in deep concentration, he appealed to the heavens and separated his palms. The ring remained suspended between his hands, as if it were floating. He made it spin and flutter gracefully, turning his fingers around it to prove it wasn't a trick. After a few seconds, Aukan closed his fists. He let out a sigh, as if he had just made an immense effort, gave Thérèse her ring back, and granted himself a silence filled with wisdom and reverence before delivering a great truth.

"Levitation is the future."

Margot was wide-eyed, astonished as never before. Spurred on by the appreciative looks of the assembled Lonsoniers, Aukan began listing the most prominent levitators in his community and among shamans and mediums, as reported by the old chroniclers of Nacimiento, unaware that as he spoke, he was inspiring the one and only obsession of Margot's life.

He spoke of his brother Huenuman who had remained suspended in midair for three days without food during a ritual, and had had to be brought down with a rope for fear of falling from hunger. Then there was the indigenous chief Rutra Rayen, whom a missionary had found hovering a cubit above ground, and who was immortalized in the stained-glass windows of a European church. He mentioned the case of two hunters who, after consuming *ibadou*, had risen so high they had flown out of sight, only to be found again hours later sitting dumb and panic-stricken at the top of an oak tree. There had also, he said, been cases of semi-levitation, optical illusions, somnambulists feigning rapture, skilful con artists playing games with magnetism, but none had struck him more than the man who, in mid trance during a procession dedicated to St. Francis of Assisi, had flown above the crowd, flying effortlessly in sandals and smock, soaring into the sky like a candle. This monk, named Joseph of Cupertino, had taken flight in front of a captivated audience of one hundred people, without anything appearing to hold him up or spur him on, simply flying alone in the face of divine biology.

"He was the first aviator," Aukan concluded.

Margot felt herself shiver. A question came to her lips before it could occur to her to stop it.

"The first what?"

These words uttered in youthful haste rang out like a prophecy. Everything from that day on was the prologue to her finding her vocation. Many years later, Aukan admitted that the ring levitation had been simply a time-worn magic trick based on nothing more than invisible thread, two balls of wax on each fingernail, and a good story. He had imagined his performance might teach her the art of illusion. Instead, he made an aviatrix of her.

After this defining encounter, the expression on Margot's face, like that of other passionate people, was a strange amalgam of intensity and blankness. Every night she waited until everyone was asleep before slipping out of her bed, opening shutters painted with water lilies and, with a sense of daring beyond her years, going out via her bedroom window. She tiptoed mouse-like along the roof, passing the skylights in the attic or the open shutters of the upper floors, making sure not to be seen from the servants' windows, going as close to the edge as possible and allowing one leg to hang off the side to feel the intoxicating sensation of vertigo. She imagined she was levitating above the city, taking flight over the banks of the river Mapocho, and she carried on gliding, spinning gracefully and nimbly in the air, circling the Catedral de Nuestra Señora de la Asunción, plunging down towards the Museo Nacional de Bellas Artes, or soaring up over the trees of the Parque Florestal to Plaza Baquedano, traveling in her imaginary airplane, floating above men and chapels like St. Joseph of Cupertino.

It was from her grandfather, Étienne Lamarthe, El Maestro, that she received her first book on aviation. It told the story of the Caudron brothers, who had dissected birds in the Somme Bay, searching for the secret of flight written inside their guts. Like her grandfather, who had always had a taste for the unusual and adventurous, Margot became an unrivaled source of aeronautical knowledge without ever having seen a metal wing. When Margot was an adolescent, Amelia Earhart became the first woman to make a solo flight across the Atlantic. From then on, she was fascinated by the recordbreaking aviatrixes of the era. She wanted to be like Maryse Hilsz, who had flown eleven thousand kilometers from Paris to Saigon aboard a Morane-Saulnier without a radio.

She followed intently Léna Bernstein's crossing from Istres to Egypt; the Duchess of Bedford flying her Fokker in a dress with a train and lace around the neckline; Amy Johnson's legendary journeys to Australia; the glory days of New Zealander Jean Batten, nicknamed the Garbo of the skies; and, of course, she knew by heart the story of Adrienne Bolland who, at the age of twenty-five, had flown over the Cordillera de los Andes without a map or navigation instruments, alone aboard a plane made of wood and canvas.

Margot no longer went out wearing a dress and an Alice band, bodice and sandals, but a leather cap topped with aviator glasses. She fashioned herself a uniform of cotton drill trousers and black boots stuffed with sheep's wool, inspired by the black-and-white photographs she had seen in El Maestro's books, and stole a gold-plated crow brooch from Delphine's collection to pin close to her heart. It was the first time in bourgeois Santiago that anyone had seen a woman walking around dressed as a man but, out of ignorance or shame, they concluded it must be a French custom. At that age, Margot had a faraway look in her eyes, but she already possessed the keenness of sight that she would later be known for when she joined the air force academy. She was an early developer but remained short and fairly plain, with thick toffee-colored hair and the beginnings of a rounded figure. She had no interest in trivial romances or ordinary matters of the heart, and soon tired of Santiago's French circles, who talked about the Roaring Twenties as if they were in Paris and attended the Obrecht sisters' "*collège des demoiselles.*"

At seventeen, she was proud to know nothing of Verlaine or Rimbaud, preferring to study the synthetic fibers used to make hot-air balloons. She read neither Gérard de Nerval nor Aloysius Bertrand, but never tired of memorizing the rainfall charts, with meteorology in its infancy. She only knew about Icarus's flight, closing the book before his fall. The sight of her already called to mind a future of tents beside runways, oxygen masks and powerful turbulence. It wasn't the thrill of the uniform, the allure of leather, the prestige and stripes that appealed to her, as to so many others. Margot Lonsonier entered the world of aviation as one might once have taken holy orders: to live and die for her vocation.

Margot

Old Lonsonier's wine business was flourishing. He no longer merely produced wine but bought it from other estates in the Valle Central to distribute to the big city markets. The Santiago of the day was home to eight hundred thousand inhabitants in eighty square kilometers. Making the most of the city's expansion, Lonsonier set up his office in Avenida Vicuña Mackenna, the closest thoroughfare to the train line, so that shipments of barrels and bottled wines from southern towns like Puente Alto and Rancagua could reach his base in the capital quickly.

Up and down the avenue, the old trades were quickly being replaced. You no longer saw the chair restorer, the tinsmith, the barrel organ player, his rolls of paper gnawed by a caged parrot. There was no sign of the watchmaker, the lamplighter with his pole, or the *sereno* singing the time and the weather. Now the Spanish had the monopoly on ironmongery and the building trade, the Turks had the post offices, the Jews the tailor's shops, the Italians the grocers. In place of the old professions, the French had brought retail outlets, improved the silverworks at Lota, established new foundries and mines in Caracoles, and ran six Grasse perfume factories which rivaled the high standards of the Provençal original.

A true man of his time, Lazare in turn decided to throw himself into the world of business, setting up a company making communion wafers on the site of a former cutlery factory. It was meters away from his home on Calle Santo Domingo – so close you could see it from the garden if you hoisted yourself up on the bars of the aviary. He bought it for peanuts when its former owner, a mustachioed man from Arica named Emiliano Romero, announced he hadn't sold a single knife since the North Americans had flooded the market with cheap industrially made products.

"They've ruined me from the blade right up to the handle," he complained, pinching his mustache between his fingers.

At the age of forty, Lazare was a sensitive gentleman who could talk knowledgeably on a range of topics. He still had trouble with his lung and sometimes suffered from migraines, chest tightness and breathing issues, but he had found the courage to calm the storms that once had shaken him. This was how he came to set up shop in the Romero factory, whose ceilings were three meters high, with long windows like those in a church and a floor made from a single piece of concrete across which grindstones had been dragged for sharpening blades, where handles had been carved from buffalo horns and where flour would now be worked in place of metal. It was a beloved sanctuary for Lazare, retaining until the day of its destruction its smell of yeast and steel, corn and fire, and would be the scene of the rise and fall of his descendants. Soon business was booming and, to his delight, the biggest churches in Santiago were on his books.

He realized chemists could make use of his wafer mixture to encase capsules, and sweet makers to cover nougat. In the space of a few weeks, he gathered more presses and humidifiers for the plates. To begin with, the machines were kept in the main hall, where a large space had been cleared for them, but soon Lazare had joined the workshop to a disused hangar via a long, narrow wing with two floors, with the ground floor devoted to the machinery and the first floor to his office. From his window, he enjoyed views over the city, and he spent an extraordinary amount of time in the light-filled room he called his "chapel." Surrounded by wafers and flour, he kept the space as quiet as possible, sitting calmly by himself as he no longer could at home, filled as the house was with aeronautical maps, boxes of food and the lingering stench of bird droppings. Far from the distractions of domestic tasks, Lazare spent his time poring over his accounts, meeting clients and fulfilling contracts, living like a hardworking hermit.

One night when he was sleeping in his office, he woke with a start to the sound of footsteps coming from the machinery room. Anxious at the thought of an intruder on the factory floor, he looked about for something to arm himself with, but all he found to defend himself was a St. Benedict cross lying on a table. He opened the door quietly, switched on all the lights at once and discovered a young thief standing at the bottom of the stairs. A skeletal figure with greasy hair and tattered clothes, the boy had sneaked into the factory to eat the wafers. Brandishing the cross, Lazare leaned over the guardrail to threaten him.

"Stay right where you are or I'll crucify you," he shouted.

He ran down the stairs to give chase, knocking several trays of flour to the floor. The thief tripped and Lazare threw himself on top of him. Just at that moment, two police officers alerted by the noise came hurrying in. At the sight of the boy pinned to the floor with the cross against his temple, they grabbed him and handcuffed him. In the drama of the moment, Lazare shouted that he would press charges and testify against the boy at trial, but the police officers jeered.

"A trial? No one's going to come looking for this kid. We'll take him round the back and deal with him."

Seeing the thief's eyes widen in fear, Lazare suddenly felt terrible. The longer he studied the boy, the weaker he appeared to be, with a wild-looking adolescent face without a trace of a beard, and olive skin he must have inherited from a distant relative in the saltpeter works.

"What's your name, boy?" he asked him.

He lowered his head.

"Hector Bracamonte."

Looking more closely at the boy's features, Lazare recognized the son of Fernandito Bracamonte, the old neighborhood water carrier who had filled the Lonsoniers' bath for more than twenty years. His hands were like his father's, with spade-like palms and black, swollen fingers. Lazare was filled with shame as he saw once again the image of Helmut Drichmann standing beside the water well, abandoned and doomed. Lazare asked the police officers to take off the handcuffs.

"Drop the charges. I'll take care of him myself."

When the officers had left, Lazare turned to Hector and placed the St. Benedict cross in his hands.

"There's a hammer in there," he said, pointing to a drawer. "Put this cross on the wall for me."

The boy went timidly to the drawer, took out the hammer along with two nails he found inside a glass, and stepped towards a wall.

"No – over there," said Lazare.

He pointed towards the staircase. Hector crept up the stairs and, when he got to the top, began to fix the cross with gentle taps of the hammer. Frowning, Lazare watched him wordlessly, staying close to the door leading out onto the street. When the cross was hung, he opened the door.

"If you want to eat, you have to work."

He picked up a dozen wafers and stuffed them into the boy's pockets before closing the door behind him. The very next day, Lazare went to Ernest Brun's shop to buy a gun. They sold him an 1892-model black revolver, slightly tarnished. That same evening, he went to the factory and hid two bags of bullets inside a red box he found high up on a shelf, untouched for years with nothing but yellowed sheets of paper and letters of condolence inside. When he put the box back, buried under crates of stuff, it occurred to him it might not be a good idea to hide the gun and ammunition in the same place, and he decided to place the gun in the inside pocket of a jacket hanging on a hook instead.

Two days later, when he opened the factory door at 7:30 a.m., he found the boy huddled in a poncho in the porch. Hector Bracamonte rose and stood before him with the look of a handsome warrior, carrying his bag under his arm, and said proudly: "If you want to work, you have to eat."

Lazare took him on as an apprentice. He soon found him to be a loyal and hardworking employee, of honest character and a reserved disposition. He came and went with brooms under his arms like a cacique, built of hard animal stuff, as if he had emerged from the belly of the factory itself. Though his eyes were hard and piercing, there was not an ounce of malice in his gaze. His eyebrows were as wild as caper bushes, his hair smooth and very black, and his lips were so full that when he smiled, his mouth stretched as wide as a concertina. He was the first and last worker in a factory he came to love as if it were his own, but it was not until many years later, in the dark days of the *coup d'état*, that he could truly thank Lazare for saving his life.

For Lazare, a period of great prosperity was just beginning. He began wearing pinstriped suits with a valerian in his buttonhole, scarves embroidered with centaurs and, as he barely went out,

Persian slippers on his feet. He grew an impressive mustache which unfurled like a rug from his lip. To his mind, there was no one better placed to represent his country, to help maintain its position and restore its prestige than a man who continued to sing the praises of the motherland from ten thousand kilometers away. And so it was that he almost never left the office. He got into the habit of eating there with his feet propped up on an open drawer, endlessly calculating the profitability of his investments, spending his nights holed up inside the factory walls surrounded by towers of papers and bills, at the top of the staircase adorned with the St. Benedict cross. As a symbol of his rebirth, he placed an elegant bunch of poppies inside a shell case bought from a secondhand dealer. He even invented a system of metal cables that meant he could lift the catch on the front door from his office, so he could let people in without leaving his chair. His clients multiplied, the contracts rolled in, the accounts improved, and to stay ahead of his competitors, Lazare became so engrossed in his business that he failed to notice that his daughter was entering adolescence.

So it was Thérèse who fulfilled the roles of mother, guardian and teacher while Lazare became ever more absent, withdrawing to his solitary kingdom of numbers where he was not to be disturbed. Sometimes he hurried across the living room to find a piece of paper, spoke a few words and rushed his dinner. Impatient and anonymous, unsmiling and distant, he became a stranger in his own home. Thérèse came to miss the days when he had been attentive and shy, hardly daring to move without asking her first; the gentle, wounded man, fragile in his cornflower-strewn bath, who had been carried in on the winds of her life like a stork which had lost its way, with his tender voice and clumsy embraces. Which was why, when Margot told her she wanted to be an aviatrix, she felt her heart sink.

"Talk to your father about that," she replied.

Lazare had reservations. He remembered the birds' invasion of the house sixteen years previously and concluded that too much of this aerial absurdity might become an atavistic trait of the family.

"Do as you wish," he told her, "but stay away from birds."

Lazare was foolish enough to leave her on her own, despite having tried his best to avoid her falling in with bad sorts. Later, looking back on his words to his daughter, he had to admit that the idea of her deciding to build a metal bird in the garden was the last thing on his mind. In the spring, after weeding a patch of the garden to make more space, she laid out a large tarpaulin and set about replicating Lindbergh's *Spirit of St. Louis* by hand. She went all over Santiago to find materials, rummaging through the secondhand and hardware stores on La Alameda, the scrapyards of El Mercado and the bins round the back of metalworking factories. The garden became gradually scattered with landing-gear beams and rectangular steering pieces. On flattened grass beside the turnips and carrots lay half a propeller, which looked as if it had been sliced in two with a sword; an upside-down wing like the lost wheel of a chariot, and, close to the vine, piles of Douglas fir timber. Thérèse eyed suspiciously the endless stream of greasy, dusty cast-offs her daughter had found lying around in dirty warehouses, now piling up on her land as if it were a junk heap. She tried only once to put her daughter off when she found her holding an ax to one of the lemon trees in front of the house, wanting to use its wood for her wings.

"Those lemons are part of our family history," she told her.

But Margot went ahead and cut into the tree trunk, making long sticks which she glued together to form the frame. She had sewn herself a dirty gray uniform which hung loosely off her body, a jumper with a propeller pattern which went down almost to her knees, and clogs with reinforced metal toes. Climbing up and down a wobbly ladder with her grease-stained arms, she looked as if she had washed up on a desert island and was building a boat in the sunshine. But she soon realized she couldn't do it all alone. She started to look for a partner who would approach the task with the same dedication and blind hope as she did, who would do a tidy job and, in return for a share of the profits, be ready to run the same risks. Word spread and within a few days, a young man turned up on a rainy Tuesday, soaked to the skin, looking like a young Cossack with dark little eyes buried behind puffy lids.

His name was Ilario Danovsky. He was a Jewish boy who lived nearby, in a house on Calle Esperanza. He said his father was a pilot. He resembled a bulldog with wide nostrils and a chubby, round, moon-like face. Early in the morning he would arrive at the Lonsoniers' in his work gear with a worried expression on his face, passing almost unnoticed as he worked tirelessly day and night to get the plane finished. It was as if an inner voice, foreseeing what fate had in store for him, was telling him to get on and live. Though he was bigger, stronger and heavier than Margot, he seemed to tire more quickly. They worked in harmony, each responding to the other's actions. A kind of knowing camaraderie developed between them, which Margot allowed for the sake of getting the job done. Their working relationship was so straightforward it left no room for ambiguity, so that Thérèse was far more concerned about her daughter's aeronautical aspirations than about Ilario's romantic intentions.

In the month of September, they attached the wings. Sitting in the middle of the garden, squeezed between the vine stock and the aviary, the plane resembled a lyre. There were tubes sticking out all over it, masts to catch the wind and an undercarriage so rigid that the wheels only turned when bathed in oil. Like the

Spirit of St. Louis, the back of the fuselage was bound in Pima cotton which Ilario had gone to great lengths to source, and which would bear the frame, covered in eight coats of aluminium paint. In Limache, El Maestro bought a cheap Anzani motorbike whose fifty-horsepower engine would propel them to take off.

One day when Thérèse heard the two of them arguing over the launch date, she went running to Lazare, who dismissed her concerns.

"Whether they try tomorrow or in ten years' time, that plane is never going to take off," he replied.

So he barely raised an eyebrow the following day when he went to fetch a cup of coffee from the living room and found his daughter wearing a fur-collared jacket and an inflatable life jacket.

"Today I'm going to fly," she announced.

Margot wedged her goggles in place with a handkerchief stuffed between her nose and the strap, then slipped her fingers into brown sheepskin flying gloves. She put on a helmet and strode out of the house to her machine, silent and focused as if heading towards a date with destiny. She was so busy preparing for every possible accident or dramatic turn of events that she had forgotten all about Ilario Danovsky, who strolled up to the door in the early hours of the morning dressed as an aviator of the 1910s, with golf trousers and tartan socks. The bold outfit was a sign of his pride in his hard work. He had even gone so far as to hide a perfectly straight parting under his hat, designed to give an impression of effortless elegance when he stepped out of the cockpit.

Four-story buildings had begun to spring up around the neighborhood alongside grand hotels and high-end casinos, but Calle Santo Domingo was still just a long road which had barely been paved, lined with wooden shingled *quintas* and posts to which horses could be tied. The police wore white uniforms and all the *esquinas* still had their stone pillars and crest of red roof tiles. Word soon reached the neighbors that the first airplane ever to be built in a garden by two adolescents was going to take off round the corner and fly over the capital. They became fired up with local pride, clearing the streets of the carts and chinchilla sellers. Market-garden stalls were set up, folded paper garlands were strung up in windows and the lampposts were decorated with yellow and black cloth, so that in the space of a few hours, before the aircraft had even been rolled out, the road looked as lovely as a sleeping bee.

Margot and Ilario wasted no time. Before the enthralled onlookers, they stepped into the cockpit and strapped themselves in. Margot was carrying out a thorough preflight check when a young journalist stepped out of the crowd and asked: "Where are you headed?"

She looked up, realizing that the only thing she hadn't thought about was the final destination. Refusing to be caught out, she thought of Adrienne Bolland and replied: "We're setting a course for Buenos Aires."

There was a round of applause. Spurred on by the spectators' enthusiasm, she explained that they would cross the cordillera, where the lowest mountain pass was at 4,300 meters altitude and the temperature was minus fifteen. In preparation, she had slathered herself in grease and onion skins, which she claimed would counteract the effects of low oxygen. She had even packed an ax in case they crashed and needed to cut off a wing for shelter.

"If it all goes wrong, we'll still land in Argentina with a bang."

The audience hailed her courage. When she eased off the brakes, they all stood as one. The engine purred, a sound so familiar it was as if it had been with her since birth. The plane shook slightly, jolting along the cobbled road, heavy with fuel, its repurposed motorbike engine shuddering. It paraded before the assembled neighbors, hopping along flea-like as children came out to see and the faithful crossed themselves as it passed.

The plane was accelerating when suddenly there was a loud bang and a sharp crack. No sooner had they begun to pick up speed than they were slowing down again. The plane was moving forward so laboriously and awkwardly that the crowd could keep up with it on foot. It spluttered, paused and stumbled absurdly on, before the engine finally gave out. The crowd continued to cheer them on, convinced that the engine's sudden silence must be a crucial step towards takeoff. But Margot alone understood that her plane was not going to fly.

She almost wished there had been some terrible accident or airborne catastrophe, so that the day would be remembered for her heroism or tragic demise. As the plane's momentum kept it rolling on without an engine, Margot realized that the road was becoming ever narrower, lined with streetlights that were coming dangerously close to the wing tips. Fearing she was about to be wedged between two lampposts, Margot braked, and the plane stopped abruptly in the middle of the road like a stubborn donkey.

Ilario turned to Margot and winced at the disappointment on her face. Feeling useless and dejected, she began to quiver with rage. She was about to get out of the cockpit when she noticed a murmur go through the crowd. The sound of music could just be made out.

A passerby exclaimed, "A fanfare for the takeoff!"

Margot unfastened her seatbelt, undid the strap under her helmet and unbuttoned her life jacket. Straining to see, she noticed first a line of women playing drums, while the men walking behind them swung trumpets from side to side. These divine, bronzed creatures with thick hair and rough hands spoke with a different accent. Behind them trailed a crowd of children with curious eyes and sandy feet, holding birds on their shoulders, wearing strange costumes as if they had stepped out of country folklore, and they began to unfurl a canvas banner woven by big-bosomed women, on which was written in large letters: *For the greatest aviatrix in Chile*.

Margot opened the cockpit and stood on the pilot's step. Just then, a man wearing a cloak and holding a baton appeared amid the players. It was none other than Étienne Lamarthe, El Maestro. He had come all the way from Limache with all his musicians and twenty-five shiny new instruments, to send his granddaughter off on her first flight.

She began to walk towards El Maestro, but he was still in character, and wrapped two thick ropes around her waist. Using carabiners, he attached the ropes to her flying harness and signaled to someone behind him. She suddenly felt herself lifted several meters off the ground by a system of lines and hoists, floating in midair. She flew over the road strewn with flowers and garlands, through the noise of fireworks and laughter, and passed over the stationary plane which had failed to take off and now lay stranded like a beached whale. It was only when she was right up in the sky that she caught sight of Aukan standing next to El Maestro and realized they had recreated the scene of St. Joseph of Cupertino levitating above the crowd. She stretched one arm out in front of her as if gripping a joystick, bent her spine as if settling into a seat, and only then did she imagine herself above the clouds, closing her eyes to allow the invisible aircraft to lift her spirits.

The Danovskys

However far back the Danovsky family tree was traced, there was a rabbi on every branch. Jacob Danovsky was the tenth in a long Ashkenazi line, the eldest of twelve boys born in a village in a dry bush-covered valley in central Ukraine, a place of grass snakes, meager pickings and superstitions. His family lived in a shtetl backing onto an Orthodox village with a wooden synagogue. The boys endured a strict education and compulsory military service which, under Tsarist Russia, meant being treated more as serf than soldier. For the past century, the Jewish population had been consigned to live in a narrow corridor in western Russia running from the Baltic to the Black Sea. Their daily lives were hard, wretched, humiliating. Their business activities were curbed, their food rationed, and, despite the small degree of influence they held, the rabbis were the first to fall in the pogroms.

The assassination of Alexander II set off an unstoppable wave of massacres and looting. Christians destroyed the Danovskys' village and burned the holy books in the synagogue, leaving them with nothing but a sad stone cemetery covered in ash and sheets of metal warped by the flames. The Danovskys left behind their home, their turnips and sage plants, to embark on a dangerous journey lasting several months, during which they slept on farms and on steppes, followed secret routes in Roma caravans surrounded by straw and beetroot, and shared licorice liqueurs with vagabonds. This was how Jacob Danovsky came to cross the continent, hop over the Channel and arrive in London, a city filled with newcomers who spoke no English and formed groups by dialect. Through Yiddish, the treasure of the Jewish diaspora, immigrants from all over Europe were invisibly joined in one sprawling network.

He married Paulina, who had come to London with a group of young pioneers from Galicia, to the north of the Carpathians. She was a tall woman with long blond hair, divorced from the father of her daughter, Aida. Their early days together in London were happy enough, but soon the difficult conditions, the pain of exile and the memory of the pogroms made them dream of another life across the ocean, on the distant shores of the New World.

Around this time, a Jewish financier by the name of the Baron de Hirsch joined forces with the visionary scientist Dr. Guillermo Loewenthal to organize a huge emigration of Russian Jews to Argentina. Word spread, reported in Odessa newspapers, that the Baron had bought a number of plantations three hundred kilometers from Buenos Aires to create a new Promised Land. After twenty centuries of oppression, one hundred and thirty Jewish families from Bessarabia, Podolia and Moldavia boarded the cargo ships *Lissabon* and *Tiolo*, which were filled with rabbis from Sebastopol and Karaites, young Talmudists from the yeshivas, and Polish sermonizers, all heading for the port of La Plata. Jacob Danovsky, Paulina and Aida crossed the Atlantic aboard one of these ships, and within her iron flanks Bernardo was born — a hesitant boy with a rather damp demeanor who would, years later, become father to Ilario.

On arrival, they took a train to the Jewish settlement of Carlos Casares, amid cold plains where the wind swept through fields of cardoons, and huts covered in roofing felt stretched as far as the eye could see. They had to start from scratch, building lodgings, choosing crops and using the swing plow, despite the fact most of the men were as inexperienced at building and bricklaying as they were at herding sheep or cows. They faced shortages of food and medicine, invasions of locusts and epidemics among the cattle. In the settlement's main square, they built a synagogue of both olive and quebracho woods, to symbolize the union of the old and new worlds. They made a cemetery without flowers or wreaths, and a rudimentary clinic with thirty or so beds, surrounded by *ranchos*. They taught their children to take the cattle out to pasture, but also to say traditional prayers. Poor and bedraggled, broken and ill, these Jewish immigrants had carried their religious customs over thousands of kilometers and transplanted them to the patch of land they had been promised, and on the first Friday of March, their shacks glowed with candlelight to celebrate the beginning of Shabbat.

Within a few months they were dressing like gauchos, drinking *mate* and carving their own *bombilla* straws, and had learned to cut the *asado* in the *criolla* way. They set up a *carabineros* post, a small stable and a bazaar where honeyed apple cakes were sold. The settlement was crowned with a school centered around the Hebrew wing where the five books of the Torah were studied. Time here was measured in slow, flipped seasons; the mountains were not those of the fables they had inherited, and the progress of this new people was not marked by a migrant's haste. At the beginning of the century, Carlos Casares had spread over forty hectares and was home to more than five hundred inhabitants. The land had been dug over, planted with Jerusalem artichokes and cabbages, beans and spinach, and black sheep were scattered over a patchwork of grazing plots on the banks of a large lagoon called Algarrobo.

Jacob, the town's rabbi, settled in one of the houses on the main square with Paulina, Aida and Bernardo. He was now an old man with a white beard, leathery hands and a body like a shriveled carob pod. He was a quiet, monotone fellow, who furrowed land and recited psalms with the same blithe cheer. He wanted Bernardo to continue the family line and become the next rabbi, but at twelve years old, his son did not follow Jewish teachings, read the Talmud or respect the sabbath. He no longer went to synagogue and gave up Yiddish in favor of Spanish. In line with tradition he underwent his bar mitzvah at the age of thirteen, reciting the necessary words and chanting along with the *teamim*, but these religious customs were the only sacrifices he was willing to make for his father's sake.

He distanced himself from the strict rules by which his ancestors had lived, and felt no sense of mission. Time inevitably eroded the old ways, and on one November Saturday, Bernardo took advantage of the fact that everyone was reciting prayers at synagogue to slip inside the bakery and stuff himself with forbidden pastries until he made himself sick. Jacob was so ashamed and furious at his son's double crime – the theft as well as the violation of a holy day – that he decided to publicly shame him by tying him to a tree in the village square with a sign around his neck: *I ate during Shabbat*.

According to Bernardo, it was on that very day that he decided to leave Carlos Casares for Santiago in Chile, where he lived from the age of fifteen until his death, though he never gave up his Argentinian nationality. He immediately became a popular member of Santiago's small Jewish community, a tight-knit group, solid as a menorah, but which welcomed external unions conducted in an open and proper way. He soon fell in love with an actress who was the daughter of Jewish immigrants, a petite woman with big blue eyes whom he met at a play at the Teatro Municipal. They were married a few months later in the Bicur Joilem synagogue at the southern end of Avenida Motta. The couple rented a tiny apartment in the Chacra Valparaíso district in the east of the city, on the top floor of a building surrounded by leafless trees, whose single window looked out over a square.

One August 21, thirty years after his father's exile, when Bernardo woke up from his siesta, he watched Frenchman César Copetta Brossio take off outside in a Voisin biplane he had readied for flight in the space of a week. The sky was within reach. Bernardo was so impressed, so fascinated by the display of progress he had witnessed that he decided to pursue a career in aviation.

However, as he weighed more than seventy kilos, was short-sighted and married, he fulfilled none of the necessary criteria for taking his pilot's exams, so had to make do with spending his days in a windowless office on the site of El Mercurio, Chile's first aeronautical organization. The years were spent drafting regulations, altitude certificates and lists of flight durations and distances. He worked with businessmen who made bold investments in this postal market of tomorrow, helping to equip the country with new airplanes and raising funds from the sands of the Atacama Desert to the snows of Punta Arenas.

When his wife fell pregnant, the couple moved to the middle-class neighborhood of Santo Domingo where many French families lived, and where their only son, Ilario Danovsky, was born. The child had jet-black eyes whose solemn, vague gaze seemed to view the world with uncomfortable sadness. As he grew older, he proved to be a shy, sweetly clumsy boy, a naïve poet of sorts. There was nothing to suggest the heroic and noble, impassioned and righteous side he would display in battle many years later, during a war in which he would play a decisive role.

At the age of sixteen, he heard that a girl in his neighborhood was looking for an assistant to help her build an airplane in her garden. Her reputation for pride, arrogance and coolness only served to increase his curiosity, and he turned up at the Lonsoniers' door without much forethought one rainy Tuesday, as round-headed and bedraggled as a wet bird. Later, he would admit he had been immediately impressed by Margot, struck by her elusive, unflappable character, her wild and direct manner. He worked harder with Margot than ever before, following the girl's lead, as her courage helped him to overcome his own reserve. He was as keen to please her as he was to attract the attention of an absent father who, at more or less the same time, had begun writing a Chilean aviation bible in which he was so absorbed that he failed to notice his son following in his footsteps.

The flying school and the Air Ministry worked with their European counterparts with the aim of training pilots in the event of another war. The prospectus said nothing about admitting women, and Ilario saw a chance to put this right. After Margot's failed takeoff attempt, this young son of a long line of travelers and promised lands, abortive utopias and difficult quests, decided to speak to his father.

Two days later, Bernardo Danovsky came to see for himself the plane they had built. He burst into the garden in green canvas trousers and a pilot's jacket and took a good look at the machine. At last he turned to face Margot and placed his hand on her shoulder.

"To think they're still raising girls to do needlework."

The following day, Margot and Ilario were admitted to a small aviation club outside the city for flying lessons. Expecting a winged kingdom, they arrived to find a warehouse. In front of them were a number of fields with three runways made of bare, bumpy earth peppered with puddles of oil. There were various run-down, industrial-looking barns. Everything was ash-gray colored, dull and dilapidated. On the roofs there were beehives, hens' nests and market gardens, while in the repair shop – as filthy as a medieval blacksmith's – an old black mare slept. There was nothing more rural and ordinary than this field of muck-rusted metal, with amateur planes gracelessly coming and going, promenading between the huts and the parking area like a procession of handcarts. There was no sense of surprise or ceremony about it. The students learned to pilot wind-battered, badly made, clapped-out craft; it was a miracle they could get them airborne.

Like Thérèse in the falconry circles of Río Clarillo, Margot had to brave lascivious looks, lewd jokes and innuendo from the mechanics, and fend off the captains who tried to seduce her with tales of daring escapes. She fought stubbornly to keep the regulation twenty centimeters of hair, which she held to as a mark of feminine dignity. After a month, she asked for her baptism by air.

One morning while she was helping to solder together pieces of a cabin, one of the instructors appeared before her, looked her quickly up and down and said: "You, tomorrow, 6 a.m."

That afternoon, she passed her medical examination – in fact, the nurses were so impressed by her lung capacity they told her she could breathe quite easily above the peaks of the cordillera if she so wished.

"You have a fine pair of lungs."

"It runs in the family," she replied.

She reported to the runway at dawn the next day to the sight of sheep wandering freely, branches strewn everywhere and a mocking note scrawled in her honor: *For Margot's takeoff*.

A weaker person than Margot would have turned around and gone home, but she simply rolled up her sleeves, took off her helmet and spent an hour picking up the sticks, biting back tears. She thought of Maryse Bastié, whose tragic and fascinating life she had read about, and how she had struggled against all the disadvantages of her sex. She had the painful sense that the only thing she had in common with the other aviators at the school was the badge she had had sewn onto her jacket. When the instructors arrived, she was standing on a clean, smooth takeoff strip, free of sheep and other hazards, ready to do what she had come for.

She was assigned a Travel Air craft barely more substantial than a motorized kite, covered in fabric and with antiquated controls. She jumped into the cockpit, adjusted the belt to her waist, carried out the usual checks and turned on the engine. A deep, modulated rumble emerged from the bowels of the plane and the propeller began turning. What had been nothing but a pile of metal, nuts and bolts just a few days earlier now began to inch forward. The runway lights were lit. The plane picked up speed and with a few hops suddenly began to climb up into the void.

She felt no vertigo or fear, only the animal force of the 500-horsepower engine lifting her off the ground and unfurling its wild wings. She flew so high she felt she could see the whole country in one go. Thick clouds broke into curving humps and lumps, rounded as vases, hanging like corals, covered with hidden veins, their shapes distinctly womanly. It struck her that the sky should not be referred to in the masculine, *el cielo*. The idea that the first aviators had been men was unbelievable to her. Seen from here, the curvaceous sky was explosively feminine. This celestial dwelling place was like a nest, a breast, proving that the first civilizations of the clouds had been matriarchal.

All the flights that followed would echo that initial journey. Margot easily obtained her pilot's license. She improved her technique, progressing more quickly than others. It was said she could touch the weathervane on a bell tower in midflight, and nosedive at two hundred kilometers an hour to lift a scarf off the ground with her wing tip. But in March, Margot realized from the clipped tone of her mother's letters that all was not well at the house on Calle Santo Domingo, which had fallen further into autumnal solitude as the leaves of each year fell. With her daughter away and her husband distant, Thérèse gradually became more and more dejected, and her slow collapse had spread to the aviary, which sensed the family's fractured state and fell into a general state of depression. Illness struck a hundred birds like a lightning bolt, leaving them weak, suffering from bouts of fever and green diarrhea, with puffy eyes and pale beaks, so that you could no longer step inside the aviary without feeling as if you were entering the room of a patient on their deathbed. The tits' heads were bowed, the sparrows were hunched, the hobby falcons' wings drooped, the budgies' feathers were ruffled and the lovebirds were racked with spasms. The grace, strength and elegance of Thérèse's owl was so depleted that it became one of those rare birds which live without feathers, covered only in pinkish skin like a damp cat.

This was the situation Aukan found when he arrived at the house, introducing himself as one of the city's finest veterinarians, carrying a suitcase filled with barbiturates and syringes. He examined the birds with hitherto unseen instruments and began extracting secretions from their beaks. Working nimbly and carefully with a constant frown, he injected herbal mixtures, drained pus and combed through plumage, occasionally pulling out lice the size of walnuts which he killed with white vinegar.

"They could eat a horse," he said.

Aukan insisted on disinfecting the whole aviary. He claimed

that isolating the sick creatures would aid their recovery, and he ordered them to be immediately taken one by one to rooms whose ventilation was adapted according to species.

"We have to create a suitable environment for each bird."

Thérèse defended herself, explaining that she had personally taken great care to draw up the list of birds which could happily cohabit, but Aukan replied with a note of concern in his voice.

"It's clear we're living in a world in which different races cannot exist side by side."

At the time, Thérèse paid little attention to Aukan's words and, though she was a well-informed woman, failed to pick up on his allusion to the situation in Europe. It was not until very late in the day that Latin American journalists began to talk about a strange character, a German chancellor who was attracting big crowds of supporters and promising to find those responsible for the economic crisis. Rumors were circulating that a war could break out, that Nazism was spreading among the most vulnerable, and this stream of reports arrived with such certainty, seemed such a foregone conclusion, that Thérèse decided it was not to be believed.

While news of the impending war was yet to reach the flying school, word did arrive of the ailing aviary. Margot decided to take a train back to the capital that evening, arriving in the dead of night a few hours later. She returned transformed by the confirmation of her vocation, by having pushed herself to her limits through the tough, athletic life at the school. At the sight of the veterinary clinic, the half-empty aviary, the smell of disinfectant, rotten food on the bird tables and birdbaths as dry as drained moats, she threw Aukan out of the house and put Thérèse to bed.

With her newfound energy, she put away the medicines scattered over the table, cleaned away stains and paid the servants, who had been demanding their wages. Wearing a mask over her mouth, she inspected every corner of the aviary and came to the difficult conclusion that the space could no longer decently house so many animals. The dazzling creatures who had once presided over this kingdom were now wizened, ragged, debased, trembling like convicts. They lifted their bald heads, tiny and powerless, with puny beaks and wrinkled quills, batting translucent eyelids.

That night, she waited under her covers for the house to fall silent, as when she used to creep out to walk on the roof. When she was sure everyone was asleep, she tiptoed out of her bed and went out into the garden in darkness. The aviary was a sorrowful sight, like a well devoid of water. Behind the dirty bars, Thérèse's owl was gasping in pain. Margot could just make out its skinny frame, its crumpled beak and swollen belly. It was staring vacantly around its abandoned home, plunged in milky darkness, like a lazaretto filled with lepers. A few little heads emerged from the bird boxes hanging from the bars, and rotten eggs which had never hatched infected the air with a fetid stench. As an aviatrix, it seemed to Margot that dying in a cage was the worst possible end, and in the pain of that moment she resolved to make a grand gesture.

"These birds are going back to France," she told herself.

She threw the door wide open and moved the most delicate birds onto the grass. Some flew off immediately, while others stayed still, huddled up, waiting. Little by little, unsettled by the movements around them, those which had remained in the cage began to flutter about, ruffling their plumage, springing out in a flurry of feathers. Margot freed a hundred birds that night, as if freeing herself from her old life, before going back to her room. During a night of restless sleep she had a nightmare in which she could see the aviary burning with green fire and *carabineros* killing the birds inside. She woke up covered in bark chips, as she had on the day of her birth, and raced to the garden to make sure the aviary was empty. But as she approached, she was astonished to find that all the birds had returned during the night, not having known where to go, and were now sitting on the roof of the cage like a head of bronze hair.

Thérèse appeared wrapped in a shawl, with a newspaper in her hand and a look of dread on her face.

"Forget the birds," she exclaimed, handing her the newspaper. "Germany has just invaded France."

Ilario

Later, as she faced the German planes, Margot Lonsonier was never quite sure why she had chosen to enlist in this war when her dual nationality and sex would have saved her from conscription. The birds' disease faded into the background, and from then on she became so consumed with the conflict that her neighbors thought she must have a new love interest. She pinned up maps to follow the movements of the Free French Forces by air, studying their progress along red dotted lines as her father had done during the First World War. She made her own flying uniform, while the young women of the neighborhood knitted scarves for the drafted troops, and every night, by the light of a yellowish bulb, she dreamed of splendid towns in faraway provinces being wiped off the map by the chaos of bombings. Not only did the newspapers *Candide*, *Jour* and *L'Illustration* bring reams of new details every week, but their Chilean counterparts *El Abecé* and *El Popular* dedicated half of their pages to coverage of events in Europe, putting information panels up outside their editorial offices which were changed so often it was hard to keep up with them.

Chile remained neutral for almost the entire duration of the conflict, limiting itself to diplomatic threats and continuing to guarantee postal deliveries from Europe even to the far south of the country. The *Fuerzas Armadas* were, in any case, equipped for all of fifteen minutes of combat. Perhaps because they lived so far away and had been the victims of disinformation, many young Chileans supported the Third Reich at the start of the war. Like Ilario Danovsky, they were convinced that the United States was lying and manipulating the press, and that Germany was trying to clean up corrupt democracies. But as the months went by, in the north of Chile, reviews and special editions like *Mi Lucha* and *Ercilla* began to circulate en masse, bringing news of Nazi atrocities and the Hitler Youth. L'Instituto Chileno Norteamericano screened free documentaries in city squares so that everyone could see what was happening on the other side of the ocean. In November, a communiqué from the Air Ministry announced that the French air force had lost three hundred planes in the space of two weeks.

At the same time, Maryse Bastié declared in the press: "Female pilots are ready and waiting to serve."

On some vague impulse, Margot heeded the call. She applied to the French embassy and sent a letter to the consulate asking for her name to be added to the list of civil pilots. Although she was old enough to sign the letter in her own right, she wanted her father to do it, symbolically giving his blessing for her to go and fight in England. But Lazare was so absorbed in his flourishing business that he barely looked up when Margot appeared before his desk, and initially mistook her for an Anglican nun come to pick up her boxes of communion wafers. Margot was a real woman now, a force to be reckoned with, and as she stood before him, he felt as if he was watching her being born for a second time.

"I'm off to fight for France," she told him.

He saw himself twenty-five years earlier, standing naked in the middle of the lemon-scented living room, holding up his fist as he uttered these same words – the words of a lost young man. At the age of forty-six, his passion for France remained as strong as it had been in his youth, but so too did his fear of war. He begged her to stay.

"If I don't go," Margot replied, "the French will send us one of those letters for cowards with a white feather inside."

"I'd rather have a white feather and a daughter than nothing at all."

But Lazare's fears were not enough to hold Margot back. She received her acceptance letter from the embassy and wrote to Ilario Danovsky, who had stayed at the flying school, to tell him she would be leaving for the front. Though she had never been to Britain before, she had done a huge amount of research, and included maps with her letter showing the position of the runways and the number and type of planes she hoped to fly.

At 7 a.m. on July 10, Ilario was waiting for her at Los Cerrillos airfield. They rose up in the sky, circled the airbase by way of goodbye, and headed for Buenos Aires, where they would join the RMS *Orbita* cargo ship bound for London.

This was the second war for a Lonsonier. By the time they arrived in London, the Luftwaffe had been bombarding the English ports for a year. Planes were attacking maritime convoys from Weymouth, the radar station at Ventnor had been put out of service and the mouth of the Thames was filling up with fuselage carcasses like an aviary littered with broken wings. Messes were set up in docks and on the outskirts of towns, with hundreds of aircrew coming and going. Saving fuel wherever they could, scorching the grass to dry it out, they had given up counting their losses. Far from home and family, Margot and Ilario soon saw that joining the Free French Forces would not be an easy matter. They spoke broken English and their Chilean qualifications were not recognized here; like all the other Latin Americans who took part in the Second World War, they had to lower their expectations.

Margot went through the phone book, calling everyone she could think of in the aviation world. Two weeks later, she was offered a position in "general services" – essentially cleaning and maintenance. Deprived, along with her fellow countrymen, of the chance of battlefield honors, Margot spent her days emptying the latrines, changing recruits' sheets, peeling carrots and digging the eyes out of potatoes. She got used to the jargon, the bombers' attitudes and colonels' whims. She managed to get a transfer to a munitions factory where she worked eleven hours a day without leave, checking the Spitfire guns. Then she was set to work washing tubes and scrubbing parts with lye, at a point in the war when Latin American recruits were joining the RAF's ranks in such numbers that the authorities decided to create a South American squadron.

As soon as her English was good enough to follow lessons, Margot was determined to complete the necessary 140 flight hours as a drogue operator to allow her to fly. She showed she could calculate positions and distances, navigate using dead reckoning and assess flight paths. She was soon called upon by the auxiliary transport ministry to play a role that would give her none of the glory, but all of the danger, in a conflict that already promised to stay long in everyone's memory. She was allowed to fly, but only moving planes from place to place. It was around this time that she and Ilario sewed Chilean flags to the shoulders of their uniforms.

She spent the next two years moving planes between airfields so that pilots could fly them into battle. When she took her first flight in British airspace, it seemed to her that the sky was less pure than it was in Chile, the stars less joyful, the horizon less open, the towns encircled by black clouds like a shepherd surrounded by his flock. Having previously only flown the innocuous, jangling aircraft at flying schools, she now found herself piloting solid, powerful machines of war, built to destroy, whose fuselage was often pocked with gunshots. Everything was light and practical apart from the huge, smooth machine-gun operating stick, which loomed in the center of the cabin like a solid mast.

At six o'clock in the morning, Margot would head to the parking zones and turn on the engines, which came rasping back to life after the chill of night. She discovered chewing gum to stop her ears from popping, learned the language of weather reports and understood you had to fly to four thousand feet to escape the constant English fog. All she brought with her were a life raft, three days' food and a Thermos of coffee. She wrapped up in furs and woollens but was careful to avoid excess weight, planing the soles of her shoes and cutting the edges off her maps.

Perhaps because she was one of the few women in a man's job, she became ever more determined not to give in to fear, that strange emotion; instead, she embraced a life of danger, showing more guts than any other pilot. She was not authorized to fire weapons, but sometimes when she was high in the sky, she let her hand run over the machine-gun stick, her muscles tensing at the touch of the forbidden object. From her rigid shoulders, stiff body and hands gripping the controls, her power and poise were obvious. She never grew tired of sitting in the same position. She flew seven days a week, nine or ten hours a day, sleeping in snatches between trips. She carried the day not through heroism, but small acts of duty. Above the clouds, she had the patience of condors who wait with lowered heads for the rain to cease.

At the same time, Ilario Danovsky was learning to fly the most temperamental craft. He was slowly beginning to understand that the success of his military career depended on his determination and bravery. He did not share Margot's taste for adventure and danger, but that only made him more eager to learn. The two Chilean friends became a close-knit team, their bond freeing them at the same time as cloistering them together. They shared the same blood, the same expressions, the same anger. While others attacked dams and bombarded research stations, they loaded planes with kit and repatriated bodies in nylon bags. Never firing a single shot, they distributed artillery parts to every squadron. They had created a kind of double act. The fatigue of one was met with the endurance of the other, and their movements were so well matched it was as if they had rehearsed them in advance.

One day, having just passed the cliffs of the French coast, they flew over a small flying school at low altitude. For a moment, Margot saw herself back at her flying club in Chile. Here were the same hangars, the same corrugated-iron huts, the same bare runways. But it took her thirty seconds to rouse herself from her reminiscences and realize that the base had been taken by the Germans.

What she saw made her blood freeze. The main field was taken up with rows and rows of tightly packed Messerschmitts, barring the way through to the land beyond. As Ilario's monoplane was close by, she signaled to him to retreat. Ilario raised his head and shivered. He had just seen three German fighter jets emerging from the clouds like black sparks, heading straight for them.

Ilario turned back towards England, charging towards the sea. He was quickly out of danger. Margot instinctively tried to do a U-turn to get away, but a Fokker starting firing behind her. For a second she could see no way out, but her strength took hold of her and, pointing the plane's nose upwards to gain altitude, Margot pulled the engine to full throttle. Two Messerschmitts roared after her. Breaking through the gray clouds, they clung to her tail, blindly flinging out bullets. There were now five or six planes all firing in loud bursts, working together to cut into her path, tracking her like an animal. Margot put both feet flat on the rudder bar and held her joystick tightly as a series of skillful maneuvers took her out of the path of the blasts. She rose ever higher, trying to scatter them, determined as an eagle, but the jets were still so close behind she could feel the breath of their propellers.

In one last effort, she did a loop-the-loop, remembering her acrobatic training, and swooped back down towards the sea. The plane was rattling all over, dancing about like a fallen leaf, spinning around as flames flew off the airfoils. The clouds began to thin. She found herself back near the coast, where she saw the flying school with its lines of Messerschmitts in the distance.

The fighter jets were so close now that she knew the battle was lost. Under attack from all sides and seeing the ground approach, she could no longer break free. But just then, she saw Ilario's plane return. Having escaped from danger, he had turned round in a sudden burst of bravery. Margot watched him heading straight for the runway of the flying school. In mid-flight, Ilario opened the cockpit, deployed his ejection seat and threw his plane down like a bomb in the middle of the German planes. The explosion was so dramatic that the fighters who had been tailing Margot turned back to help their comrades.

Columns of smoke rose a thousand feet into the air. Amid the fumes, Margot could see Ilario on the end of a parachute falling slowly towards a group of German soldiers who had escaped the flames and were waiting for him on the ground. She could only look on helplessly as he fell. Ilario tried to take out his pistol to avoid handing himself over to the enemy alive, but he found himself unarmed. He tried to direct his parachute towards the pebbly lookouts of a limestone cliff, but his straps were tangled and he couldn't change his trajectory. The Germans were still standing with their faces turned to the sky. Stranded in his flight suit, Ilario let out a scream that tore through the air and reached Margot's ears. He must be despairing, she thought. At that moment, she faced the same dilemma her father, Lazare Lonsonier, had faced in his encounter with Helmut Drichmann: commit a crime, or an act of cowardice?

Alone in her cockpit, forced to make a decision, she choked back tears. With a heavy heart, she turned her guns towards Ilario and closed her trembling fist over the firing stick, where it set rigid as stone. She put her finger to the trigger, ready to kill the only man she had loved like a brother. She was about to fire when from the end of his parachute, Ilario turned his chubby face and little Cossack eyes towards her and smiled. Within a split second, everything seemed to fall into place. His final gesture was to motion to her to leave, to save herself, not to have to carry the weight of a crime. The war would not defeat them. He lifted his fist high in the sky and, as he fell towards his death, he touched the Chilean flag they had stitched on their shoulders together.

Helmut Drichmann

When Lazare Lonsonier met him again, Helmut Drichmann had been dead for thirty years. Those who saw it happen remembered it was around two o'clock when they found the German soldier inexplicably inside the house, whose doors and windows were shut. He walked casually across the hall and sat down opposite Lazare, who immediately recognized him and put down the book he had been reading. The memory of a young, blond, ox-like figure with his face covered in camouflage mud had remained imprinted on Lazare's mind, and he was not surprised to find him exactly as he had left him in the middle of the First World War, eighteen years old, composed, square-headed with tufts of white-blond hair, matching the image he had retained of him. He realized at once that the time had come to confront the ghost who had haunted his dreams since his return from the front, a soldier who was both comrade and enemy, the only man on earth who knew his secret.

"It's my lung, isn't it?" Lazare asked, his voice hoarse.

The soldier smiled serenely back at him.

"It's your lung. You've got a month."

Helmut Drichmann had arrived from the hereafter wearing army uniform, canvas trousers with a vertical fold ironed in, and an old *Totenkopf* badge, a metal skull and crossbones the German hussars pinned to their buttonholes. All he carried with him was an empty tinplate bucket hanging sadly from the crook of his arm. He was perhaps one of the most handsome men ever to be seen on Calle Santo Domingo. His toned adolescent body contrasted with Lazare's thickened, slumped frame, aged by thirty years of restless nights, withered illusions and haunted desires. With his symmetrical features, deep, blazing eyes and Roman nose, he looked like a solid, calm and resolute young man, not a bluish, nebulous apparition come to haunt the living.

When Thérèse appeared in the living room loaded with sacks of sesame seeds and corn kernels, she was so surprised at the sight of the stranger in her home that she dropped the bags, sending their contents flying all over the carpet. Helmut Drichmann knelt down and, with patience and care Thérèse had not seen since her falconry days in Río Clarillo, carefully collected the seeds in his bucket. As Lazare looked on in surprise, Helmut stood up and headed out into the garden towards the aviary. Through the window, they watched him pass his arm through the diamond-shaped holes in the grille to feed the zebra finches, who ate straight from his hand despite being unused to visitors.

"Who is that boy?" Thérèse asked, startled.

Lazare hastily made up a lie.

"He's the son of a friend from the south."

"And why is he dressed as a German soldier?"

"I think he's not all there," he replied.

For thirty days, they told everyone who passed through the house on Calle Santo Domingo that the young man was the eldest son of a mysterious old friend Lazare had met around Cajón del Maipo during his journey with the indigenous tribe selling silver jewelry. Nobody asked questions and within a week they had all grown used to the calming presence of this young interloper, who they said must have been traumatized by a war long ago, and who went about minding his own business, observing the world with dewy-eyed astonishment as if he had just woken from a long sleep.

This was how a dead man came to join the Lonsonier family, on which he would leave a spectacular and terrible mark the following month. His arrival in May was a breath of fresh air, diluting the tensions left by Margot's absence. He appeared from nowhere every morning with military diligence, making no sound as he entered the room, barely eating, and staring at the aviary with naïve curiosity. This was no ghost wandering the house, hiding among the camellias, sneaking under the sheets like a sly spirit, but a charming and peaceable person who made his excuses before leaving the room. Though his uniform was old, it didn't smell so. In response to people's questions, he had no past, no hopes for the future, and often his only reply was an innocent smile and a slight shrug, as if death had forbidden him from speaking about the affairs of the living. Sometimes the servants blushingly waited for him in the kitchen doorway, won over by this calm, strong, attractive prince whose noble bearing filled every room with Germanic elegance.

Lazare liked him at once. He had always known death would come to him through this young soldier. His presence had been with him for so long, staying so diligently by his side, that there was a kind of understanding between them. But since he had been able to see him, an invisible underground force had been awakened, and now, a few weeks from the end, Lazare had never felt so young. The certainty that his time was up gave him a strange vitality that shielded him from grief. From then on, he devoted himself to concluding all his unfinished business, happy in the knowledge he would be dying several years earlier than he thought.

"What a relief," he said to himself. "Everyone ought to know when they're going to die."

At the age of fifty-one, robust and smartly dressed, he became the envy of the town. From now on, clinging to his youth, he wore only brand-new moccasins, a checked tweed jacket, a fashionable English aftershave and beard oils. Slight osteoarthritis meant he walked with a *bec-de-corbin* cane and kept eye drops in his pocket, but thanks to the discipline and determination he put into his work, he kept the rebellious air of those who don't wish to grow old. He wrote his will in formal, outdated French and left the running of the factory to Hector Bracamonte who, remembering how he had first entered the building, felt as if he were stealing it for the second time.

Thérèse was now at the peak of her charms. She was forty-four years old and her kindly, loving Occitanian air made others immediately warm to her. Though she had the tender look of a faded flower, she belonged to the category of women whose figure and facial structure keep them true to their youth despite the passing years.

Yet she was consumed by one constant worry. She had not heard from Margot for several months and waited impatiently for the armistice. Having lived through periods of light and darkness, she was resigned to having been born in a warring century, but she could not reconcile herself to the thought of losing her only child. As she waited to see her again, she filled Margot's room with the scent of magnolias, changed the bedsheets, dusted the aviation books still lying on the shelves and lit blue candles to hasten her return. She could not rest for a single moment, with only Helmut Drichmann's spectral presence to pull her from her torment. With his silent toing and froing between the living room and aviary, his strange way of watching the water running from the fountain and carefully looking for little kernels of corn in the feeders, he behaved like a young ornithologist who shared Thérèse's passions.

"He's got birds in his soul, too," she told Lazare one day.

Thérèse was so touched by this boy sent from the sky that she scattered the garden with containers filled with a mixture of pine nuts for doves, cereals and egg mash, so that he could offer them through the interlaced bars of the cage from his open palm. The day she saw him twisting his arm to feed the sparrows, she opened the door to the aviary for him.

"You can go in if you like."

Helmut Drichmann sat at the foot of the little fountain, tipped his bucket to one side, and filled it up. And he stayed inside the aviary, keeping the trench of his memory topped up with water, until the morning peace was declared in Europe and Margot Lonsonier was able to come home.

Margot appeared unannounced in the garden in June. She had aged like a stone, gray and rough, gaunt and burnt out, with an ache in her neck which had plagued her for the past four years. The person who came to the door of the house on Santo Domingo was a ruin of a woman. Thérèse stopped digging in the courtyard, horrified at the sight of this girl with blue circles under her eyes, a deathly mouth and pale and nervy face. A hundred times she had imagined her daughter crashing into the Channel, and now the many humiliations Margot had faced, her years of broken sleep in cramped dormitories, were written on the young woman's face.

"*Cristo santo,*" Thérèse exclaimed. "What has the world done to you?"

Until her death, Margot's memories of her return would remain vague, but she would never forget the moment Helmut Drichmann entered her life, sitting in the middle of the aviary. She was crossing the garden when she caught sight of him between the bars. She didn't notice his sadness, confusion or solitude, only the *Totenkopf*, which brought the agony of the war flooding back to her.

"*Pucha*," she cried. "We're putting up Germans now?"

As Helmut Drichmann rose politely to his feet, she saw he was a good head taller than her. For a moment, Margot seethed, only just restraining herself from punching him in the face and calling him a Nazi. But she said nothing then, nor for the nine months that followed, only breaking her silence to announce the name she had chosen for her son.

Though she tried her best to return to normal life, whenever Margot thought of England she was assailed by memories of Ilario. Images jumbled together in her head of their war work as well as shared moments of joy, and she clung to the wild hope that a messenger would one day appear to tell her he was somehow alive. She worked with pilots in Santiago for a while. Despite her talent, she was now reduced to putting on displays, spreading propaganda, flying banners attached to the back of planes or dropping leaflets, obstructing the roads with seas of paper. The return to calm, everyday life, to the ordinary distractions of a city like Santiago, felt so dull and uneventful that she was thrown into a disarray which her family's best efforts could not overcome.

Only Lazare understood what she was going through, having experienced the same thing thirty years earlier, and it was he who shyly suggested: "It's not a plane you need, it's a man."

Yet too little time had passed since her return to Chile for another man to take the place Ilario Danovsky had occupied for so long. When she closed her eyes, she could still see him falling into the clutches of the Germans, crowned by his parachute like a king, touching the flag they had sewn to their shoulders as the drone of fighter jets echoed around. It was this memory, dwelt upon often, which gave her the idea to repair their old plane, whose rusted frame still lay abandoned beside the house like a wrecked ship. With patience and discipline, she grafted away, drawing on the lessons she had learned during the war. She worked so slowly that people wondered if she spent the night undoing the day's work in order not to get over Ilario but to keep his memory alive. Sometimes when Thérèse watched her from the balcony, she sighed deeply.

"It's as if the greatest accident of her life is never to have had one."

Margot didn't know how far she would take the plane repairs, but the sound of clanging tools ended up catching the attention of Helmut Drichmann. She realized he was watching her with a look of silent concern from the aviary at the other end of the garden, like a frightened animal fascinated as much by her as by this new metallic bird. Recognizing the smell of mud, old boots and rain, she knew Helmut Drichmann was passing by as silently and blankly as a shadow, bucket in hand, and was distracted from her work.

A month went by. On the evening of Lazare's death, they ate a coq au vin Thérèse had prepared. At the end of the meal, Margot slipped quietly into her room and lay down under the quilt. She went to sleep quickly, but within a few minutes she was woken by a jingling sound. To begin with she could not tell where it was coming from, but when she leaned out of the window, she saw a faint glimmer in the darkness between the trees. Casting her mind back to this night much later, she could not say what had led her to open the shutters, as in her childhood days of rooftop dreaming, and go out into the sleeping garden, walking barefoot on her tiptoes in her percale nightdress.

The house was quiet. The lights were off. Mobiles hanging from the bars of the cage and fruits growing in the kitchen garden swayed in the breeze. The aviary was calm, the birds asleep on colored ropes strung from side to side. The nightingales had made their nests in the corners and the prince-like Java sparrows sharpened their beaks against the grilles. Everything was bathed in blue light and Margot had the sense that something special was happening. She stopped to look around her, taking in the beauty of the scene, all the elements of which had come together in a picture of strange, timeless perfection.

Looking up at her plane, she saw a figure framed by the cabin window, then Helmut Drichmann's head buried among the controls, where he was repairing the instrument panel. He looked paler, more diaphanous than usual, with his shining eyes, fine white eyebrows and ivory forehead. Then she heard his voice, quiet and melancholy as if coming from another time.

"I know why this plane never took off."

Helmut Drichmann no longer seemed an irrational being, a ghost come to wander this forgotten corner of the earth; having studied him properly, she saw that something in his profile had changed slightly. He took off his serge jacket and rolled up the sleeves of his wool shirt. She went to step back, but he leaned down to kiss her.

Margot felt as if her lips were touching the skin of an enormous snake. She felt the chill of his frozen veins, and when he pulled her against him, it was like stepping inside a block of ice. And yet she let her body relax, threw her head back, opened her thighs and held on to the wings of her plane. She clung on tighter, covering her mouth with her hand to stop herself waking the neighbors as a brute force tore through her like a spear, making her bend double and almost breaking her in two. She made no attempt to fight the ferocious pleasure, the metallic passion of the moment, her eyes glued to Helmut Drichmann with an expression of both defiance and submission.

They made love only once, and despite his prowess, Margot had the strange feeling it was his first time. She had given him in death what the young soldier, taken too soon, had never known in life. It was a nebulous yet entirely fulfilling kind of pleasure, which moved to the rhythm of the birds' constant flight across the aviary and the scent of dry engine oil. Margot's shameful passion for Helmut Drichmann was probably the most dreamlike emotion she felt in her life, more intense even than flying over the aviation school, and half a century later she would still summon the memory to fill her lonely nights.

While Margot was experiencing her first night of love, Lazare was savoring his last. He had tried his best to act naturally all day, working with his usual discipline, and no one noticed anything to suggest he had been told of his impending demise. He bore the fact disconcertingly serenely, as though preparing to receive a great honor. That evening, he tidied his "chapel," filed his invoices and, as he left the factory, slowly turned out the lights, filled with nostalgia as he breathed in the smell of flour for the last time. He felt slightly unsettled but was almost immediately flooded with a deep sense of relief, of deliverance, as if he had been waiting for this moment since birth.

In his bedroom, he found Thérèse naked, lying in the bath, floating in the water like an undine. To him, she was still as radiant as she had been on their wedding night, when they had loved one another amid the scent of cornflowers and coriander. Gone were the wedding dress, the amber molasses and all other forms of artifice: they had reached the age when love requires autumnal simplicity. Here was a woman whose body was as fragile as a bird's foot, whose hips were no longer firm nor her bottom perfectly round, and who was fixing him with a painfully trusting look. A new kind of nudity was taking shape. He joined her in the warm water, pushing all his memories up to the surface, and kissed her lightly so as not to break the delicate balance she had created. Knowing he was already dead, without warning her of the sadness to come, Lazare had the shameful sense of having understood his wife far too late. As he lay peacefully against her, their bodies entwined in the bath, he whispered these last words which she would never understand.

"I killed Helmut Drichmann."

When Thérèse awoke the next morning, Lazare was no longer breathing. She stayed a moment in his cold embrace, staring into his motionless face, and his eyes now dark like two wells, empty but for a frozen glimmer that sent shivers down her spine.

At three in the afternoon, they perfumed his body with myrrh. Slowly, gently and achingly tenderly, Thérèse put him into the pinstriped suit whose buttonhole he liked to adorn with freshly picked valerian, and rubbed a sweet-smelling oil into his beard, taking even more care of his appearance than he had done himself. She was surprised at how thin and wizened he looked, as if death had carried part of him away. Just last night in the bath, she had held a strong, powerful man in her arms; now he was reduced to a dry, hollow stone, his bones protruding through the skin of his back, his chest marked with ugly purple scars. After fifty-one years of ambition and rebellion, of shared life and fruitless pain, Lazare's body bore the marks of a long fight he had put his heart, soul and single lung into. She put a little brilliantine in his hair and brushed it back, revealing his veined, slightly greenish forehead. She plumped up the six embroidered cushions propping up his neck and gave him one last loving kiss, half faded by time. Seeing him like this, dressed as smartly as if he were going to a wedding, arms crossed over his belly, as the scent of myrrh wafted around, he looked more handsome than the man she had known.

"Even death suits you," she murmured.

They kept vigil over the body in their room, which had been transformed into a kind of gothic niche with light gauze curtains in dark colors and muslin drapes, and candles set out on the bedside table as if on an altar. The next day, as a fine rain fell, the cortege silently crossed Calle Santo Domingo, with its double row of poplars and streetlamps, where Margot had tried to fly her plane. Some of the passersby recognized her as they stepped out of their porches, tipping their hats in respect. She was silent throughout the ceremony, her eyes red and skin pale. She could hardly believe that in the space of a month she had lost the two men who had been most important to her, and given her virtue to a third. She decided to keep quiet about Helmut Drichmann, just as her father had kept the scene at the water well to himself for thirty years. But her silence only made her feel more alone, and she struggled to sleep for the first two weeks, constantly waking to a nauseating smell of wine.

Her period was late. When she realized she was pregnant, Margot's thoughts turned straight to the bittersweet memory of Helmut Drichmann, and she began counting the days on her fingers. Having been made an orphan and a mother at once, she was torn by conflicting emotions. The German soldier had killed her father and left her with a baby. The paradox was unnerving. As she was not known to have been with anyone, when her belly began to show, a rumor went round that it was the war itself that had got her pregnant. And at the end of the second month, Margot became a radical pacifist, avoiding pilots' banquets and veterans' dinners. Her tendency towards silence and isolation became ever more pronounced. She began to think she was not destined for a life in the skies, for air battles or flying airmail services. From then on she never set foot on an airfield, could no longer stand the smell of castor oil, avoided the sound of propellers, forbade anyone from uttering the words "landing" or "cockpit" in her presence, and she was almost shamefully happy to lose her vocation as a pilot forever.

In the absence of Lazare and Ilario Danovsky, her attentions turned to the hardworking Hector Bracamonte. Left in charge of the factory at the age of thirty, with his tanned skin he still had the air of a hard-grafting peasant, a quiet blacksmith, and his experience and self-confidence showed him to be ever more trustworthy. He tried to follow in Lazare's footsteps and grow a mustache, but had to make do with an unimpressive shadow of fuzz. He tried to compensate for his failed facial hair with a stiff voice and a sense of authority that made him seem more mature and considered. He was outwardly serious and a man of few words, but applied himself to his new job with missionary zeal and devotion. Seeing him at the helm of a flourishing business, fulfilling his role with integrity and fairness, very few people could have predicted he would one day be seen curled up on the ground, kicked and dragged like a dog, offering his life in place of another's.

He led by example, never letting the business go into decline. He pushed his former colleagues to be more productive, aware of the lazier workers' ruses, and his experienced eye saw through every shortcoming, caught out every idle moment, allowed no slacking. With the workers, he was friendly but strict. Knowing the strengths and weaknesses of his men, he hoped to show them that they were capable of more than they knew. But he soon detected a change in their attitude towards him. Since his arrival at the factory as an adolescent, he had lived among these hard and stubborn men, for whom standing up to authority was a badge of honor. After Lazare's death, they demanded improved working conditions, cleaner toilets and gutters and a longer lunch break. In their eyes, Hector was no longer just another pawn, but the severe, intransigent master they dreaded. His abrupt coronation raised their hackles. He fought fiercely against this change of atmosphere, but it soon became clear that the battle against hearsay had been lost before it began.

A strike was called. The motors of the kneading machines were stopped, the pump rollers were left to go cold and orders for thirty truckfuls of flour went undelivered. The wafer factory was plunged into cathedral-like silence. Another kind of multitude was rising up. Younger, more recent recruits wearing red shirts and starry caps demanded reforms and suspended all activities to signal their discontent. They held rattles and horns, old saucepans and cowbells, and even a little drum fashioned in haste from a cheese box and two knotted laces. The strikers made such a din that Margot was roused from her bedroom. When she arrived on the factory floor, she saw that all the machines had been turned off. The men were standing around with arms folded, and the most rebellious among them, red-faced with anger, threatened to build barricades of bags of earth, to bar the doors and windows and turn the factory into a medieval fortress.

At eight months and three weeks pregnant, Margot listened to the heated arguments from the sidelines. The catcalls and drumming drowned out words. All the workers were raising their arms, railing against Hector, when all of a sudden she heard a deep, cavernous roar, which seemed to come from the depths of the earth. She thought at first it was the sound of someone shouting across the factory, but soon realized it was coming from her own belly and that the child, woken by the commotion, was now clamoring to make his arrival in the world.

The energy in the room swiftly changed from factory strike to a scrum of midwives. The workers ran about trying to find a car, making way for Thérèse who had heard the child's alarming call from the living room, and one of the men, a giant from the coast, was asked to carry Margot in his arms because yellowish waters were already beginning to run down between her legs onto the floor. Later, Margot would remember rushing into the hospital, screaming, her dress already unbuttoned, her chest covered in red patches, banging on the walls like a madwoman, her belly warped by lumps and rifts. Despite her adventurous spirit, when the time came to give birth on the hospital bed, she was bent double. The midwives came running, bringing basins and towels. When Margot began to push, her eyes filled with tears, and the sound of her pelvic bones dislocating could be heard from the corridor, as if an oak tree were being uprooted. The child tore through her guts, kicking, impatient to live, and he wriggled so hard to get out that Margot felt as if she were giving birth to an ox.

The child was born bottom first, his legs stretched out along his torso, feet pressed to his ears. The newborn was placed on his mother's chest. Margot, naked, covered in sweat, panting and exhausted, clutched this purple, bloodied creature between her breasts, hair slicked to his head and little fists grabbing at the air as if trying to throttle it. Though the child was shriveled and small, like a horrible lump of flesh, his eyes were already open, and he studied his surroundings with unnerving curiosity which reminded Margot of his strange paternity. The child was examined and found to have a birthmark on his right knee, typical of rebellious people.

"This child will kneel before no one," she said.

The birth was registered with the Chilean authorities, but also at the consulate as a French citizen born overseas, a fact which, twenty-seven years later, was to save his life. She gave up on the idea of giving him his father's name, convinced that its Germanic origins would expose him to prejudice. She thought of giving him a more fashionable French forename, but was afraid to destine him to follow in a line of uprooted people. And so she chose the only name that still echoed around her heart, simple and powerful, which suddenly appeared to her like the most obvious thing in the world, and her family raised no objection. The boy was named Ilario, and to differentiate him from Danovsky, she added a contraction: Ilario Da.

Hector Bracamonte

The year Ilario Da was born, old Lonsonier would celebrate his ninety-first birthday. Despite the ravages of time, loneliness and exhausting harvests, he refused to die. Strong and tough, he boasted of still being able to swim naked in the icy lagoon some evenings, diving into its depths to visit his late wife. From his farm in Santa Carolina, he looked on impassively as the family births and deaths kept coming, and nothing seemed to distract him from making wine. In January, Lonsonier had given new life to his production by turning to less industrial forms of farming, inspired by French postwar practices designed to rediscover the alchemy between palate and plant. To protect his crop, he surrounded the vines with fig trees, offering the birds worthless fruits to tempt them away from the grapes, and followed his own set of rules involving filtering the grape must and varying the sulfate content. Such was his situation when he heard that his granddaughter Margot had given birth to a boy. He left his vineyard, his stone cellar and his lake, boarded a train carrying a case of his finest *cru*, and walked into the living room on Santo Domingo a few hours later, robust as an acacia, to fill his great-grandson's bottle with his first taste of wine.

"I don't need to write a will to pass on this inheritance," he said.

No one questioned where the baby had come from. He looked so much like Margot that everyone agreed she must have had him on her own. Yet, while Margot had been a quiet, reserved sort of child, Ilario Da was noisy, flamboyant and quarrelsome. Indeed he was so loud that when the neighbors heard him crying theatrically all through the night, they feared he might end up becoming a singer. When he was still a babe in a rattan basket, he was extremely alert, pointing to a thousand objects a minute, sleeping with his eyes open, and his muscles developed so quickly that he was walking before he even crawled. Everyone thought the child's voiceless power, self-assurance and hidden strength were early signs of a passionate character, while only Margot worried that Ilario's insatiable energy foreshadowed a complicated life ahead.

Ilario Da grew up in the sheltered world of the wafer factory, which had its own set of rules and laws, at a time when Santiago was still a safe city, free of denunciation and terror. Thanks to Hector, the factory floor soon became a place of calm and safety for him. He was raised amid the scent of flour and piles of wheat, of wool grease and dust, moisture and dough presses, his ears attuned to the buzz of machinery and the workers' curses. He learned to say Hector's name before Margot's and would call it shyly but eagerly, not knowing that he would continue to invoke it until his very last breath, at the end of a life of battle and torment, for only the man who had broken his way into his family by the back door, who had come from a long line of West Indians and prophets, who had known nothing but the hierarchy of a factory, only this Hector with the saltpeter face embodied the bravery and dignity he would always strive to imitate.

Four years after Lazare's death, Hector Bracamonte had finally cemented his new position and transformed the business into a kind of cooperative. With no father or grandfather to look up to, Ilario Da worshipped Hector instead. He would lie on the sacks of flour piled up in the warehouse under the giant nave of the main hall, breathing in the smell of wet dough. This was how he came to hear of anarchy as freedom, of the people's bank, the history of the Mapuche indigenous resistance and the Red Cavalry. When he asked to hear the story of the massacre at Santa Maria de Iquique for the tenth time, Hector Bracamonte told him he would be better off watching and learning how to work tirelessly, methodically and with discipline.

"The greatest battles are won on the ground," he said.

Hector loved the child like his own, though he never let it show. Kisses were replaced by manly silences; maternal indulgence gave way to chores; instead of cuddles came demands and duties. It was as if there was a kind of pact, man to man, between the gruff worker and the illegitimate child, each somehow warmed by the coldness of the other, each fully aware of his duty for commitment at both extremities of life. The Marxist working-class love with which he was raised made Ilario Da a tough and intelligent child, content to live without fulsome feelings, who would continue to avoid unnecessary displays of affection and to shun a woman's touch until the end of his days.

He made impiety his religion. He ate out of a mess tin like the workers: boiled vegetables, four eggs in the morning and huge amounts of stodgy *choclo*. He learned to survive the winter without complaint, and to refuse all privileges. At the age of six, in Margot's arms he watched a march in support of a young socialist presidential candidate, Salvador Allende, who lost to General Ibañez. The memory of the event marked him so deeply that he resolved never to give in to the lure of wealth or luxury, and it was around the time of this first taste of mass uprisings that his dislike of hierarchy and admiration for oppressed peoples took permanent root in him.

At the age of nine, there would have been nothing to distinguish him from any other French boy in Chile were it not for the secret of his mystical blood. When he was very young, Margot could see a resemblance to Helmut Drichmann's pale, square face, but when she saw her son playing bare-chested in the garden, paying no attention to the birds in the aviary, she understood at once that the only thing he had inherited from his father was his sex.

One day on the way home from school, he asked his mother: "Who is my papa?"

Margot told herself that everyone, even children, had the right to know the truth. So she replied as honestly as she could.

"I am."

Ilario Da's parentage was never discussed again, and when asked he would say his father and mother were one and the same person. His childhood was played out amid workers' meetings around the holy wafers and monthly visits from Aukan, who skipped in laden with stories, rejuvenated by his adventures, bathed in the unusual scent of cool citrus zest, his pockets filled with herbal candy, little bags of corn and marzipan sweets. This man of many talents and a dazzling way with words had grown tired of traipsing around ignorant regions with his magic, tired of wasting his art on poachers of hens and pumas, tired of plying his trade at sorcery markets. He had decided to settle in Santiago in a little house on the edge of the city to which he invited Ilario Da, unpacking the coffers of his imagination in a room filled with calfskin-bound volumes which had crossed the cordillera on muleback. He described to him a world of female warriors, a world where giants turned into wooden statues and girls were born among flaming sugar canes.

When Ilario Da asked him where this land of wonders was, Aukan pointed at the bookcase behind him and, gesticulating wildly, exclaimed: "It's a land you can find in books."

It was he who taught the child to read and write, first in Mapuche, whose grammar he considered fundamental, and then in Spanish when he realized the boy was easily smart enough to master both an ancient language and a newer one. Ilario Da was soon able to draw the letters of the alphabet with a steady hand, writing with religious deference with a clean goose quill and an ivory inkwell. When he had finished forming his first word, he read it aloud with theatrical flourish: *Revolución*. He shut himself away in his bedroom to copy it out again in big letters, covering several sheets of paper, staining the carpet with black ink spots, filling notebooks with these ten prophetic letters which did not yet sing to him of glory as they would one day soon. Margot kept these pages, with their huge, clumsy characters, in a little red box stored away upstairs at the factory, on a shelf in Lazare's chapel, until the dictatorship uncovered them twenty years later.

At twelve years old, Ilario Da was so scrawny that when he lost a few grams he looked as if he might disappear altogether. He began to grow at an alarming rate, yet still did not gain weight, so that the slender frame he had once been able to hide became all too horribly clear to see. At thirteen, he was five foot four and weighed seven stone. He was as tall and thin as the country itself. His muscles were delicately entwined like blackcurrant stems and, though he was still more of a child than an adult, Margot decided the time was right to introduce him to his great-grandfather.

They left for Limache one Sunday in September to meet El Maestro. But Étienne Lamarthe never had the chance to get to know his great-grandson, because he died that very afternoon, trumpet in hand, surrounded by his instruments and twenty students during a Bellini rehearsal in the private rooms of the regional administration. He had been following a rather frugal diet made up of grains and carrots, honeyed walnuts and raw fish, and spending his days adapting libretti and listening to recordings of famous operas. The tanned, adventurous young reveler who had crossed an ocean with thirty-three instruments in a trunk had become a spectral figure with gauzy hair, slightly hunched from a lifetime of bending over his music stand, suffering from bouts of sudden tiredness that made him stop in the street and cling to the nearest lamppost.

On the day of his death, he was conducting. With one hand on the music stand and his baton in the other, he had reached the third movement when he heard the final call sounding in his chest. Then silence fell inside him as a velvet curtain closed before his eyes, and he felt for the first time as if he were embarking on a piece without knowing the score. He let nothing show and had the grace to continue with the rest of the rehearsal, so that none of the players in the pit noticed that El Maestro's heart had stopped beating. At the end of the rehearsal, he collapsed onstage. In the chaos that followed, he was carried to his house and laid down in his modest bedroom, where the word on the street was already being whispered: *"El Maestro se está muriendo."*

With his head propped up on five pillows, Étienne Lamarthe asked for his trumpet. He brought it to his mouth, but his wizened and useless lung could only play an awful note, a hoarse sound, a dull lament which instantly brought home the gravity of his condition. He let out one last sigh, clenched his fists, strained his ear towards a distant melody, and his eyes closed as his lips formed a mischievous smile.

At the same time, Margot and Ilario Da arrived in the town square, which was being paved. In the middle of the square, surrounded by walls of colorful posters and three-story buildings, the bust of Vincenzo Bellini still stood on its plinth, the wind blowing through the Chuquicamata copper curls cast for El Maestro's concert sixty years earlier.

Two men were lifting the statue and Margot, suddenly struck by a premonition, said in a broken voice: *"El Maestro ha muerto."*

For nine days, a long queue stretched in front of the house, as every inhabitant of Limache took the time to pay their respects. Beside the four-poster bed, as Ilario Da stood gazing at El Maestro's ivory profile, it seemed to him that his great-grandfather had the same pale face that was imprinted on the wafers at the factory. He was too young and knew his relative too little to mourn his loss, but he was polite enough not to say anything during the whole ceremony, patiently watching the funeral which would provide material for the short story he would write a week later.

Margot, on the other hand, kept vigil beside him all through the night, and shed more tears for him than she had for her own father. Suddenly the image she held of this supportive grandfather, perhaps the one and only man who had always believed in her inventive spirit, was no more. She was surprised to find him looking so small, wizened and old, with only his messy hair and Sétois seafaring looks to testify to his past. She gently lifted the collar of his jacket, whispering to him softly as she stroked his brow and adjusted the bow tie which had been put round his neck for his final journey. She looked on in horror as the body was moved from the bed to a gold-studded coffin, and it was only once he was peacefully ensconced inside with his baton in his hands that Bellini's head was placed in there with him, like a biblical relic, so that the Sicilian could lie with the man who had taken his music as far as the skirts of the cordillera.

The whole village joined the grand funeral procession in honor of the sole composer in Limache's history, but not a single note was played. To commemorate the man who had made the loudest sounds ever heard in the region, they had decided to maintain a dignified silence, accompanying the casket without fanfare, and in the absence of music everyone remained strangely alert for the next fortnight. He was buried beneath a hillock opposite the cemetery rather than inside the graveyard itself, as if to place him somewhere between heaven and earth, and his headstone was simply inscribed with the word "Maestro" and a golden G clef. Two days later in the main square, the Bellini statue was replaced with his own bust.

The next day, Ilario Da awoke with the burning desire to recount what he had seen in a notebook Aukan had given him. His first lines were composed as a simple diversion, but writing soon became a source of pleasure, then a kind of compulsion. He had barely begun to write when characters began to throng into the cathedral of his mind as if arriving for a party, forming an entire land of fables and battles, and expanding this world came so joyfully and easily to him that he found himself filling the next page before he had finished the one before. His handwriting was small and dense, almost jammed together as if racing to move forward, with long tails on the "p"s and "q"s and towers rising from the "l"s and "d"s. There were no loops or curves, but tall, slender capitals, swords and crossing points, as if his pen were sped by the ardor of his blood.

At the age of eighteen, he had adopted the look of a serious existentialist, with a checked felted coat and a cigarette permanently hanging from his mouth, his breath thick with the day's seventeen coffees. He could spend hours on a single detail of a story without losing the overall thread, and drew on an endless supply of plot twists. He had an orator's skill for captivating an audience and a fortune-teller's knack for manipulation. He could pause the action, create narrative tension, contain a character's emotions so as not to break the flow, explain without telling, find a device to reignite the story, and create such a realistic setting that the reader felt as if he or she were really there.

At university, he made a weekly wall newspaper which served as an information panel for the students. Thick, strong hairs grew on his chin and chest like steel wool. He grew a brown mustache, tobacco-yellowed at the tips, and became as fascinated by politics as artists usually are by art.

It was around this time that he met Pedro Clavel, a militant in the MIR, the Venezuelan Revolutionary Left Movement. He was an energetic brown-haired man with protruding bones and ocher skin and a fine mane of hair, whose calloused hands and cratered skin attested to years spent in tropical sierras. He had adopted Castroist teachings at the end of Perez Jimenez's dictatorship, fought for agricultural reforms despite not being a farmer, miraculously escaped execution in Nicaragua, and all his experiences, as stirring as they were dangerous, had instilled in him a combative faith that became ever deeper and more serious as time went by.

Ilario Da met him in a café known as Rincón Caliente, where a group of young activists, Cuban socialists and Argentine militants met every Thursday afternoon to debate the copper miners' strike, the truck drivers' walkout and attempts at social destabilization around bottles of wine and empanadas. One morning, deep in a discussion on authoritarian liberalism, Ilario Da followed Pedro Clavel to his house in a suburb of Santiago. Pedro lived in an outbuilding at the back of a yard filled with pigs and rabbits. He showed off the three humble bookshelves above his bed, filled with loose sheets and hastily written letters on coded papers. He spoke about his family in Maracaïbo, his wife Céleste and his beautiful sister named Venezuela, whose path would cross that of Ilario Da many years later in Paris.

Then the conversation moved on to the danger of a dictatorship of liberals and the importance of being ready for all eventualities. He was a model of intelligence and courage, and when he spoke sionately about his past struggles, Ilario Da was impressed by his modesty. At that time, young militants were passing around Nikolai Ostrovsky's book *How the Steel Was Tempered*, published in Santiago with a cover made of card that had already been used on one side, so that turning it over you found snippets of old account ledgers. Pedro Clavel's only copy had become a compact pile of dog-eared, annotated paper, a monument of pages browned by rain and squashed mosquitoes, which he handed to Ilario Da with Soviet solemnity.

"We need men like you in the party," he told him.

Ilario Da could not hide his surprise.

"What party?"

"The MIR," Pedro Clavel replied, lowering his voice.

And so Ilario Da joined the MIR, which advocated the dictatorship of the proletariat and the emancipation of the working classes. He joined this new family with a mixture of amazement and trust, and silently swore to uphold the party's aims for the rest of his life. He quit his university course and joined another school of men and women with a different kind of discourse, where they spoke about cooperatives, minimum wages, retirement and paid holidays. He let his hair grow, revisited the treasures of Bolshevik culture and exhumed forgotten artists buried by the old republics, doing his best to seize a political moment he felt, in his ignorance, was destined to make history. He would arrive home at all hours in a leather jacket and red T-shirt, baseball cap and long boots, with a resolute air that earned him the nickname Pantera. Enthusiastically breaking down every barrier his class put in front of him, he let his unwashed curls fall messily down over the obstinate brow where the seeds of a lifetime of commitment were already forming.

"That boy's going to end up a Marxist," the old ladies in his neighborhood would exclaim.

*

In September 1970, President Allende came to power. His victory had such an impact that, for the first time, the face of another youth was seen on the streets, holding up ancestral *palines*, signs and placards as they came to celebrate the historic moment when the voice of the people had drowned out that of the oligarchs. Along with half the country, Ilario Da and Pedro Clavel joined the crowds gathering beneath the balcony of La Moneda, where the people's president was standing wearing a simple suit and a sash over his shoulder. Soon forty-seven factories were nationalized and credit was made more accessible. Agricultural reforms led to the expropriation of more than ten million hectares of fertile land; there was full employment, a rise in salaries, and in a single democratic act, the Unidad Popular seized the copper mines from exploitation by North American businesses.

Ilario Da could not hide his joy at spending countless sleepless nights criticizing the *capitalist system* – words which rang out like a diabolical order, sprawling, flawed, imposed; words which had not only to be combatted, but rewritten.

He often spent Sundays with Margot, who had become a hippie with colored plaits and baggy clothes, a bohemian whom life had left penniless, her neck adorned with seeded necklaces and her wrists loaded with bracelets. There was little trace left of the wild, flamboyant aviatrix of yesteryear, who had grown up in military schools and fought in Europe with the RAF. In winter, she organized pacifist meetings in her living room, hosting a dozen former colleagues like a congregation of monks. One day, Margot was surprised to see a smartly dressed elderly man among them, who appeared to be carrying the weight of the world on his shoulders. He had a thick mop of white hair, powdery skin and the permanently confused look of the rootless.

It was Bernardo Danovsky who, thirty years on from his son's death, was such a shell of his former self that there was almost nothing left of the man Margot had met in her garden all those years ago. Since then he had been working at Tobalaba airdrome on a vast exposed field in the suburb of La Reina, where Los Cerrillos flying club had been moved after its closure. It was such a huge space with so many facilities that there were not enough planes to fill it. Margot welcomed him warmly, and from then on Bernardo Danovsky attended every *tertulia* she organized, always bringing bunches of red begonias which he said made the room smell like a runway.

One evening when they were taking a walk around the garden, Bernardo came across the homemade airplane his son had built with his own hands. He was so moved by it that he suggested to Margot it be transferred to one of the hangars at Tobalaba airdrome, to protect its memory.

"Who knows?" he said. "Maybe one day it will fly."

A lorry came to pick up the plane and Margot personally oversaw its installation in one of the air sheds, where it sat in darkness for several years until it was brought out illegally for its final flight.

The prediction that Ilario Da would kneel before no one was gradually being borne out. But when it came to politics, Margot and her son never saw eye to eye. They clashed constantly. Margot was in favor of the idea of peaceful dissent. She had come to believe that war was a European creation and Chile a peaceful paradise. She had no inkling that the same violence could be committed here in the heart of the legendary country she loved best of all, as on the other side of the ocean. Ilario Da would jeer that you could not change a system through the system itself. Revolutions didn't happen at the ballot box.

"It's a semantic contradiction," he declared.

As they talked through the night, they became bogged down in arguments and muddled points. Ilario Da was excessively eloquent and Margot too worldly-wise, and the conversation took different paths but always led them to the same conclusions. They would fall silent, exhausted from having swum so far to return to the same shore, each of them convinced that history would be on their side.

But one afternoon, Margot could not help shuddering as she told her son: "If something happens, promise me you'll go to France and find your great-great-uncle."

She added: "His name is Michel René."

Meanwhile, Hector Bracamonte had stopped by the factory to look for an old invoice. He was searching through Lazare's things when, inside the pocket of a jacket hanging from a nail, he chanced upon the revolver Lazare had bought from Ernest Brun back when Hector had tried to rob him. Leaving it untouched, he returned calmly to the factory floor. Just then, Thérèse came running in, visibly shaken.

"*Están bombardeando la Moneda*," she cried.

For the past hour, a military junta had been bombarding Plaza de la Constitución and news would seep out later that Salvador Allende, locked inside the presidential palace with a gun gifted by Fidel Castro, had killed himself while the coppery notes of his voice still rang out on the radio. Officers of the putsch were said to have lined up to fire shots into his body one by one like some macabre ceremony, the last man disfiguring his face with the butt of his rifle. At the end of September he was laid to rest in his coffin with his face wrapped in a shroud and no one, not even his wife, was allowed to see beneath it. The precision and expertise of the aerial attack surprised everyone. Investigations soon indicated it had been led by groups of American acrobatic pilots who had flown to the Chilean coast as part of Operation Unitas, and that the architect of the attack had been Henry Kissinger, who was awarded the Nobel Peace Prize a few years later.

In the days that followed, helicopters circled above the poor districts of Santiago. The city was invaded by a new class of men in military uniforms, by tanks and armored vehicles, parades and flags. In the space of a few weeks, they had eliminated all known trade union leaders, slaughtered their socialist opponents and broken up all the leftist parties and, reading *El Mercurio* one morning, Chileans learned that the National Congress and municipal councils had been dissolved. Post-curfew, the *carabineros* kicked down doors, hauled couples on the endless junta blacklists out of bed and disappeared them. Teenagers were found on wasteland with three bullets in their back, while others were killed outside a grocer's in the middle of the street. Fighter jets flew over the whole country, busloads of *carabineros* tracked communists across town, and houses were emptied of books, while the new leaders paraded themselves in the press wearing sunglasses, sitting in the living rooms of La Moneda, chests covered with medals and stripes, settling in for seventeen years of dictatorship.

Chile became a land of arrests, summary executions and show trials. The DINA (secret police) searched universities, libraries and research labs, deporting the brightest minds. Three thousand assassinations, thirty thousand political prisoners, twenty-five thousand exiled students, two hundred thousand workers dismissed. The prisons were filled with emeritus professors, intellectuals, musicians and artists. The wine estates were turned into interrogation centers where poets, bakers, violin makers and puppeteers were tortured. Walking the streets after dark was forbidden, having long hair was a crime, reading poetry was suspect. They wanted to build a windmill but outlawed the wind.

Ilario Da entered a world of daily denunciations. The dictatorship held his comrades in its grip, with little room for resistance. They printed hastily typed underground tracts with bleeding ink and unpoetic headlines. The word "Allende" was used like a lucky charm, like an amulet they hung round their necks, savoring its syllables over and over again with suppressed rage. Never has Chile fought a battle as honorable as that which was played out in the country's backyards, where clandestine parties met in secret rooms and pamphlets were written in cellars. He discovered Santiago's hidden veins, its alleyways and secret passages, and amused himself by taking shortcuts home, practicing in case he needed to escape from the police one day. His dual identity as a bourgeois and militant was both frightening and exciting. Hidden behind his mask, he belonged to this shimmering city of faceless fighters, this nation of hidden weapons, this fraternity of strangers united by a bond more sacred than family. There was no better match for his age and inexplicable insouciance than this underground network of shelters and hidden doorways, where young people threw themselves into the resistance – risking torture, prison and exile – as courageously as the first aviators blindly boarding their planes, trusting their lives to the heavens.

One Friday in early December at around three in the afternoon, well before the curfew, Hector Bracamonte was startled by a series of loud knocks at the factory door. A group of five men got out of two vans without license plates and barged onto the factory floor, where they began searching the machines and the ovens in which the wafers were cooked. Two of them, in plain clothes, ordered everyone to get out their identity papers and gather in the middle of the room. Ilario Da held out his documents but a soldier stared him in the face, not even bothering to look down.

"You're in the MIR, aren't you?"

"The what?" Ilario Da found himself saying.

The man led him towards the assembled group of workers. A lieutenant with close-cropped hair and sunglasses appeared from one of the vans and began lazily sorting through identity cards.

He was in combat uniform, without helmet or belt, and khaki boots which came up to his knees. Although the tension was palpable, there was an atmosphere of false cordiality and the *carabineros* appeared largely uninterested in the exhausted men dragged from their work. The lieutenant gave orders to go through every trunk, drawer and cupboard, to move machines and sacks of flour in search of evidence. After a few minutes, two soldiers returned with Margot's red box.

"Do you have a warrant?" asked Ilario Da.

The lieutenant barely moved his lips.

"I ask the questions around here."

He wasted no time in opening the box. Inside he found the paper on which Ilario Da had written the word "*Revolución*" twenty years earlier. At the bottom, he found the two bags of bullets from Ernest Brun's shop.

"I see there are children in this house," he said, lifting up the bags. "Whose are these?"

Ilario Da went pale. He was about to speak when Hector Bracamonte cut him off.

"Mine."

"Where did you get them?"

"They were a Christmas present," he replied.

The lieutenant clenched his jaw. It was hard to pinpoint the exact moment anger rose to his face. Without warning, he stepped two centimeters in front of Hector and elbowed him sharply in the jaw. Hector fell to the ground, blood spurting from his face as several of his teeth flew to the other side of the room. The lieutenant beat him wildly in the pit of his stomach, possessed by the rage that had suddenly taken hold of him. Hector curled up, wrapping his arms around his head. Workers tried to step in to defend him and threats and punches were thrown in all directions. They were pushed back against the wall and forced to stand still with their legs apart while guns were pointed at their temples and rough hands searched their pockets and emptied their wallets.

When they realized that the factory backed onto a house, several men crossed the low fence onto Santo Domingo. Thérèse was in the middle of the garden filling the bird feeders in her aviary with oats. When she saw the *carabineros* coming towards her, at first she thought there must have been an accident. But she soon realized something else was afoot when two soldiers, following orders barked from the backyard, dragged her from the bird boxes and forced her to lie down with her hands behind her neck.

"Don't try anything stupid," they told her.

The lieutenant appeared and knelt beside her.

"Are your birds communist, Señora?"

Thérèse lifted her chin towards the lieutenant and met his arrogant stare. He pulled a pistol from his belt and shot through the grill at the first bird to approach. The whole aviary was thrown into panic. Thérèse's owl threw back its wings, eyelids curling, lifting a dust of flowers and dry bark as it fell, a bullet through its head and a trail of acid blood running down its feathers. The lieutenant returned to her side.

"Tell me everything you know," he whispered.

In a state of shock, Thérèse stared back at him, her eyes filled with tears.

"Your loss," he said. "Kill them all."

In the mauve light of the old vine, two *carabineros* armed with submachine guns opened fire. In the ten-minute massacre that followed, all the birds the Lonsonier family had collected over the years fell one by one. Bodies went tumbling to the ground amid the gun smoke, the birds' screeches drowning out Thérèse's cries as she blocked her ears with her hands, powerless. When there was not a single living animal left inside the aviary, the men turned on their heels and left the garden.

Ilario Da was praying against the wall when the first shot rang out. Hearing another flurry of bullets, he imagined the worst. It was clear that painful days were coming, but what he did not yet know was that the bullet which had killed Thérèse's owl, exploding its brain and turning its pupils white, would also drive his grandmother slowly mad. He was pistol-whipped and dragged out towards the trucks. They were about to leave when Hector, bloody-mouthed but admirably calm, asked if he could fetch his jacket from his office.

"Want to bring your toothbrush too?" one of the soldiers asked.

"It's my right," Hector replied.

"Be quick."

He went upstairs and reappeared two minutes later holding Lazare's jacket with the revolver hidden inside. Outside, the two trucks were waiting with their doors open, guarded front and back by armed men. Thrown inside one of them, Hector and Ilario Da were greeted by a rancid stench and another prisoner already sitting against the right-hand window, his neck covered in blood. Ilario Da sat in the middle and Hector against the left-hand door, behind the driver.

The lieutenant got into the front passenger seat. Hector's totemic face showed no sign of emotion. It was only when the lieutenant went to buckle his seatbelt that Hector took the gun out of his jacket and, catching him off guard, fired into his ear.

A thunderous noise ripped round the vehicle. Blood and brain spurted over the dashboard. The impact thrust the lieutenant's head against the window. Hector lowered the gun and fired again between the lieutenant's legs. His testicles exploded like two balloons, turning the seat red. The driver, who had not yet started the engine, turned around and threw himself at Hector. He grabbed hold of his arm and managed to turn the gun back on him. Winning the struggle, he pressed the revolver against Hector's brow and fired.

A red line ran down the middle of Hector's handsome face and one last victorious expression flickered in his eyes. He smiled, his face covered in blood, his shirt soaked, and with that his twenty years in the service of the man he had once tried to rob came to an end. His body was hurriedly hauled from the truck and hidden under a thick sheet inside another car, and he was not seen again until the day his body was found at the bottom of the ocean, attached to a train rail, his beautiful saltpeter profile gnawed away by crustaceans.

Around five o'clock, as Hector was being killed inside a truck, Margot was finishing a cup of mint tea poured by Bernardo Danovsky. She had no idea her entire aviary had just been massacred, her mother still kneeling before it in disbelief, and would never forgive herself for not having been there. The minute she left Bernardo Danovsky's house, she was struck by how quiet the streets were, and was surprised to see a group of neighbors gathered outside her house. As a woman stepped towards her, Margot sensed something terrible had happened.

"They've taken Ilario Da," she said.

At the same time, at the military hospital, several young detainees were queuing up against the wall when a group of soldiers burst into the room. Ilario Da heard them stop behind him and pull off a length of sticky tape which they used to blindfold him. He felt a strong pressure bearing down on his eyelids and nose as the cold plastic skin met his face.

"Close your eyes and don't try to open them unless you want to say goodbye to your eyelashes."

He was forced into another car. Ilario Da suspected they had left the capital because the vehicle seemed to be bumping along the rough tarmac of a country road. Then they stopped, the door opened and someone dragged him out by his hair. With his arms handcuffed behind his back, unable to protect himself, he fell head first to the ground and was kicked back to his feet. The soldiers made him walk without alerting him to obstacles in his path, so that for several long minutes he stumbled blindly into walls, scraping his shoulders on barbed wire and shards of glass, until he was thrown onto a damp mattress. Five men laid into him with bludgeons. Ilario Da rolled up in a ball, shielding his head between his legs, sucking in his stomach, clenching his fists so hard that his nails dug into his palms, withstanding every blow as blood drooled from his mouth.

When the beating slowed, he took advantage of the momentary let up to shout: "This has nothing to do with me!"

These were his first words uttered under torture and, as he spoke them, he promised himself he would keep repeating them to the end.

"We know you're with the MIR, fucking traitor!"

"I don't know what you're talking about."

"Señor!" one of them screamed in his ear. "You'll call me señor!"

He was about to respond when he suddenly felt a thousand needles piercing his arm and making his whole body twitch, as if he had been thrown into a nest of vipers.

"Here's what's waiting for you if you don't talk," said a voice.

He had just been given his first electric shock at elbow-level. A powerful current had passed through his skeleton like a shard of crystal, an ordeal the fear of which would haunt him for the rest of his imprisonment.

"None of this has anything to do with me, señor."

As a second shock went through his navel, he felt he was being torn apart, with bolts of electricity running from his feet to his scalp. His trousers were pulled off and he found himself naked. The cold metal electrode was brought close to his shriveled penis. He tried to pull back but before he could do anything, he felt the current on the glans. He thought his testicles would explode. His penis swelled up like a bell. He let out a terrible cry, arching his back, spreading his toes, sticking out his tongue like a hanged man, flaring his nostrils and clenching his buttocks hard. He felt as if his joints had been dislocated, his bones had broken through his skin, every hair on his head and body had been scorched, his teeth had been smashed and his eyes had popped out of their sockets. The shock lasted four seconds, then his body landed back on the ground, inert, a trickle of blood running down his penis. He was in so much pain that through his blindfold, in the darkness into which the dictatorship had thrown him, he thought he saw Hector Bracamonte floating in a kind of pure light, levitating like an indigenous angel in a dreamlike sky filled with condors and communion wafers, but he remained on the ground trembling as he waited for the next shock to come.

His hair was cut off with rusty scissors. His scalp bled. Then he listened as a document was read out describing an arsenal of clandestine weapons and likely addresses of young communists.

"I've never heard any of this before, señor," Ilario Da stammered, dry-mouthed.

This time the electrode was applied to the wounds on his head. The flesh smoked. Ilario Da screamed, thrashing around, kicking at random. After an hour, when he still hadn't talked, they got him to his feet. He could barely stand, dribbling and bleeding all over. The silence was unnerving.

Then he heard: "We'll cut it off if you don't talk."

Ilario Da felt the same rusty scissors used to cut his hair gripping his penis. One of the points was pricking his left testicle and the two blades were already digging into the base. His face was slapped to one side.

"Gonna keep playing the hero without a dick, are you? Don't be an idiot. What kind of woman's going to want you? Think about it. Don't follow what you've read in pamphlets, or the friends who are ratting on you right now in the other cells. Don't be an idiot. We'll cut it off."

The scissors were squeezed and Ilario Da began to cry – small, sporadic whimpers to begin with, and then he felt something break inside him. It was his turn to be gripped by the dilemma every generation of Lonsoniers had faced before him. The only way he could avoid being tortured into confessing everything he knew, the only way to survive was to put all the blame on Hector. It was not a matter of betraying him, but of taking advantage of the crime the soldiers had themselves committed and turning it back in his own favor. He realized then they would never let him go until he gave them a name, and even tarnishing the memory of the man he had most admired might not set him free. Making a false confession for which he would never forgive himself, he sobbed: "Hector Bracamonte knew everything."

The torturers waited, applying more and more pressure to the scissors, until Ilario Da's youth was destroyed forever, his manly dignity reduced to dust.

"We'll leave you to have a little think," one of them said, pulling the scissors away.

Four soldiers pulled him to his feet.

"Outside, dog."

They handed him the trousers of a detainee who had died that morning, ripped from the waist to the knees and covered in hard patches of dried excrement. They forced him to duck to pass through low-ceilinged tunnels and to descend winding, wobbly staircases four steps at a time. A metal door opened and as the cold air hit him, he knew he must have come into a courtyard. A punch to the stomach made him bend double. He fell to his knees, unable to breathe, spraining his right arm. With the dirty trousers, handcuffs and an old wool sweater, his body was being tugged and pinched all over. He was so thirsty he could no longer swallow his saliva and his mouth was filled with the acid taste of vomit.

Someone walked behind him. His handcuffs were replaced with a cheaper length of coir string which bound his wrists and ankles, passing between his legs. A soldier whispered in his ear: "Dead or alive, this Hector guy will get you nowhere."

Ilario Da

After Hector Bracamonte was killed and Ilario Da arrested, Margot aged overnight. As soon as the dead birds were removed from the aviary, she shut herself in her room and spent the next three days burning her son's books in the first Lonsonier's capacious bathtub, fearing the soldiers would be back to search the house. Seeing the thick plumes of smoke, Thérèse felt her daughter was destroying the last of the family's history, just as she had done with the lemon trees while building her plane, but once again she failed to put Margot off.

"You'll send all our memories up in smoke," she said. "Our legacy will be a pile of ashes."

Convinced Ilario Da had been shot by the junta, Margot covered the living-room windows with muslin drapes and only left the house to go out into the garden. Weighed down by long, dusty ponchos, her eyes red with tears, she concluded that an austral curse had fallen on the last three generations of the family, and when a man with copper bracelets and a wool headband turned up on Santo Domingo one afternoon, she didn't see him coming. It was three in the afternoon. Margot was still in bed, buried under a mountain of tissues and embroidered wedding cushions, when Aukan – of whom they had heard nothing since Ilario Da was a child – pushed open the door unbidden. He had ridden all through the night from Concepción on horseback, carrying urgent news from a prophetic dream.

"*Ilario Da está vivo,*" he said. "I saw him in my sleep."

These words, uttered with the unimpeachable clarity of dream science, went straight to her heart. It was not that she believed in *machi* omens or was superstitious about nocturnal revelations, but Aukan's certainty proved to her that she must rise from the ashes to save her son from the flames. She went to the French embassy to ask them to exert diplomatic pressure, but the ministry was reluctant to step in when they learned Ilario Da had committed a crime and the junta had found two bags of bullets in the red box at the factory. And so she threw off her hippie ponchos, ceased her nighttime wandering and became a fighter again, as in her days of tackling German planes over the shores of the Channel. She battled so tirelessly she gained something of a militant reputation, making Thérèse worry the *carabineros* would come knocking a second time.

By now Thérèse's skin was as lined as a lizard's and her teeth had gone brown; her back was curved bridge-like from her years in the aviary, and her lavish locks had thinned, now falling as straight as the needles of a monkey puzzle tree. Her resting expression had a severity that made her look hawkish and tired, the epitome of a very old woman, and her years of suppressed melancholy rose to the surface. When she was handed a plate of chicken and carrots one lunchtime, she pushed it away in disgust.

"I don't eat birds," she said.

From that day on, she refused to eat anything but gruel and ground maize out of little porcelain saucers. No one appeared to notice that she had started sucking her thumb again, as if slowly returning to her distant childhood, and when her few friends thought she seemed downhearted, they assumed the political situation was making her nostalgic. She alone understood, in a flash of lucidity, that she was gradually losing her mind. On sunny mornings, looking out of the window from old Lonsonier's rocking chair, she sometimes found herself calling Ilario Da's name as if he were still in the garden, then, realizing her mistake, would burst into idiotic laughter. Seeing her mother stray into the swamp of madness, Margot, still entrenched in negotiations with the embassy, decided to advertise for a nurse.

The following Monday, Célia Filomena arrived wearing a perfectly ironed skirt and knee-high white socks, carrying a small case filled with changes of clothes as well as tourniquets, bandages and compresses. She had not yet seen twenty but had a tenacious air about her that made her seem older. She put her things down confidently in the living room as if she had lived there all her life, and remained by Thérèse's side until her last breath. She washed her with essential oils of Roman chamomile, cooked her *brazos de reina* made with liters of *dulce de leche*, cleaned the rooms, leaving the scent of cut grass behind her, and read her Ilario Da's clumsy writing before bed. She was so devoted to Thérèse that Margot ended up wondering if the two women had somehow already known one another. Yet nothing seemed to stop Thérèse from spending hours staring out of her window at the empty aviary within whose bloodstained bars the memories of her best years were contained. It was Célia Filomena who, having understood the situation, stopped Margot one day as she was preparing to head to the embassy.

"We need to buy her a bird," she advised.

Just as the owl's crate had once been brought to the house, so now a wrought-iron cage decorated with stucco arabesques arrived holding a white cockatoo fifty centimeters tall whose crystalline crest, slicked back like the hair of a tango singer, stood up in tufts on top of its head when they put music on. It came from the turbulent rivers of Indonesia and, while its call resembled a mysterious island language, it was so attached to Thérèse it might have been born meters from her house. But the appearance of this magnificent creature who could speak, purr like a cat and roar with laughter did nothing to rouse her interest. Thérèse remained sitting in her rattan chair in the furthest corner of the room, staring at her abandoned garden, and at all hours of the day and night, filled little bowls with a mixture of canary seed, pumpkin seed and rolled oats. She began taking baths in the old tub which she had brought to the foot of her bed, and for more than two weeks, Célia Filomena was charged with filling it with hot water and rubbing Thérèse's back with a flannel soaked in amber molasses.

"My lung hurts," she groaned from time to time.

The young nurse imagined that the best way to help her was to recreate the aviary she had once known. And so for the first time since the glory days of Santo Domingo, the house was once again filled with birds from all corners of the world, slipping through checks on the railway or hidden inside luggage on the high seas. This time, however, the nest boxes were not hung in the aviary nor in the living room, but right inside Thérèse's bedroom, where she lay in sylvan silence in the cornflower-scented water of her claw-foot bath, watching dozens of birds fly around her.

Yet there was no improvement in her condition. Her mind continued its slow slide into the abyss, and she became so thin she looked like a little glass nightingale nesting among her bedsheets. Then Thérèse was struck down with a painful cough, as in her childhood in Limache. One afternoon when Thérèse was exhausted from coughing and complaining of a raging sore throat, Célia Filomena, who had learned the medicinal properties of good cooking from her mother, decided to make her a chicken-foot and horehound broth.

Having searched every drawer in the kitchen to no avail, she climbed onto a stool to reach the back of the shelves. She pulled out a biscuit tin which seemed to have gone untouched for years and found some old chicken bones inside. In fact they were Aukan's Patagonian dinosaur relics, hidden forty years earlier when he had come to tell his stories of levitation. That day, Célia unwittingly simmered up a prehistoric fossil broth so delicious that when she served it with a trickle of oil, Thérèse picked up the little bones and sucked them, never suspecting she was drinking right to the marrow of seventy million years of life on earth.

No one ever really knew if it was the dinosaur fossils or the innumerable birds flying around the room, but a few hours later, Thérèse was carried off on a paleontological journey filled with fabulous animals, curling up under her quilt like a rhinoceros in a bath of sand, and she felt so free in her wanderings, so weightless in her hallucinations, so filled with primitive force she thought she was flying. Suddenly the condor she had seen on the summits of the cordillera appeared before her in a halo of light and walked around the aviary, spreading its giant wings and letting out an operatic squawk.

She cried with happiness for the first time in years and said, in the clear voice which had made her famous before the epidemic in Limache: "There's no such person as Michel René."

This confession, which would be her last utterance, was incomprehensible to the only person in the house to hear it. Célia Filomena put it down to senile delirium and that Sunday night, she was the single witness to the death of Thérèse Lamarthe, who left this world beside her empty aviary. She was buried alongside Lazare in the Cementerio General inside a coffin lowered by four men with marine ropes, in a tomb completely covered in sunflowers on which the birds came to sit until the last Lonsonier went into exile.

*

Soon after his arrest, Ilario Da reached the torture center where he was to spend the darkest hours of his youth. In those days, Villa Grimaldi was still just a shadowy park. Rows of cells were lined up like log cabins, a hole in the roof the only window on the outside world. The huts were reinforced with planks of wood, barbed wire and metal debris, with prisoners packed together in darkness like corn in a crib. A sad state of inertia hung over this flowerless garden enclosed by a recently built green brick wall connected neither to the past nor the future.

On arrival, Ilario Da was thrown out of the car and kicked in the back as a colonel standing in front of him declared: "We get mutes talking here."

A burst of machine-gun fire made him jump, then he was dragged to one of the jails. Despite his blindfold, Ilario Da could sense the room was packed. He was made to sit and as the soldier went to leave, he turned the key in the padlock and shouted: "Who's the boss?"

"You're the boss!" the prisoners chorused.

Ilario Da was surprised to hear so many voices around him, but even more so by how obediently they behaved – proof of the hold the soldiers had over them. He leaned his head against the wall and, through a small opening at the bottom of his blindfold, cast his eyes around the room. At a glance, the space appeared to be about four meters long and two wide, too narrow for the sixteen people he managed to count around him. The walls were covered in peeling blue paintwork, and an ugly bare light bulb hanging from the middle of the ceiling was left on all night. Six chairs lined up against the wall were the only furniture besides wood-bottomed bunk beds on either side of the room.

He studied the dejected faces of the young inmates, most of them broken-boned, weary, their heads hanging, the skin of their shackled hands turned mauve. Legs spread around a pool of saliva, dirty-clothed and long-bearded, their entire bodies seemed crippled by defeats, humiliations and punishments. Some had serious burns, others deep cuts. Every time the guards passed through, there was always one who broke the silence to ask plaintively: *"Agua, por favor."*

The electric shocks made them thirsty. After an hour of quiet, a faint sound could be heard at the other end of the cell. To begin with, Ilario Da thought a group of soldiers must have infiltrated the cell, hiding among the prisoners and pretending to have a conversation for the purpose of extracting information. When no one stopped them, the murmuring grew louder and more confident and a third voice joined in. Footsteps were heard in the corridor and the room fell quiet again.

"Who spoke?" asked the guard.

No one responded.

"392, was it you?"

"No, boss."

"Then it must have been your girlfriend."

Sitting next to 392 was a long-haired young man of about eighteen whose chest, red with the blood of past tortures, was visible through his ripped shirt. The guard pulled him out of the room by the neck and closed the door behind him. Barely two minutes had passed before a scream rang out. From inside the cell, they could hear him being beaten and shocked. He clung desperately to his alibi, repeating the same excuse, giving names that failed to satisfy his tormentors, probably because they were in exile or already dead. They found out several days later that the young man had been subjected to the grille technique, which consisted of tying the body to a metal bedframe whose feet were attached to electric cables, and passing electric shocks through the anus, between the toes, under the armpits and into the corners of the eyes. The boy denied everything, his links with the resistance, his membership in the MIR, his contacts with the masterminds of the movement. The session went on for five hours.

Torment followed torment throughout the day. Ilario Da withstood all the torture, out of pride or vanity, or perhaps because he had resigned himself to the idea of laying the blame for everything on Hector Bracamonte, whom he feared would judge him from the afterlife. The prison carved hard lines on his face. After a few weeks of incarceration, the attractive, confident young man he had been in his years in Santo Domingo had become a broken, craggy-faced adult. His skin was dull and reddened and his once voluminous hair had become fine and brittle. Nothing remained of his mother's fire nor of his father's brazen youth. At Villa Grimaldi, he was halfway between an animal and a corpse.

Inside the hut, prisoner 392 was always in charge of handing out water using a little cup filled from a jug beside the cell door. He followed a set order, as if there was a secret hierarchy among the prisoners, and poured slowly, holding the edges of the cup with his other hand so that as little as possible was wasted. It took a long time to go around to everyone, but they all waited in respectful silence, to the point that they could hear every drop slipping down their neighbor's throat. When they had all had a drink, they were told to sleep. Some of them were entitled to bunk beds, others pushed two chairs together, but the majority slept piled on top of one another like sea lions, head resting on someone's knees, feet on another person's back. Their bodies all ached, their tongues were dry and their bellies were empty, and despite the solidarity between the detainees, despite the unity of oppressed peoples, it was every man for himself.

The next day, the guards reminded them of their orders. No talking, no calling out, no complaining. In short, they were to sit on a chair or on the floor for eighteen hours, waiting for their next torture session. Meals were served on the very table on which they were electrocuted. Still blindfolded, sitting in a row divided into six groups, heads bowed, forbidden from uttering a single word, they ate a vile mixture of the guards' leftovers, olive stones, old chicken bones, mandarin skins, pieces of cartilage and chewed grains of rice, boiled up in a big stock pot. From then until the end of his life, Ilario Da repeated at every meal that you could eat anything if you were hungry enough.

Little by little, disobeying the guards, the detainees began to impose their own rules. They quickly switched places, for no real reason other than to add some variety to their day. When they were sure it was safe to do so, they exchanged a few words through gritted teeth. Ilario Da realized he was surrounded by men just like him – students, lecturers, university professors, lawyers, shopkeepers – all of them ready to sign anything to go into exile, anywhere, to face any kind of odyssey to get out of Chile. They were prisoners of war, *prigués*, as they called them, who would spend their youth in the prisons of Rancagua, Linares and Talca, teaching each other mathematics, English literature, astrophysics and Scandinavian languages until their liberation, their lessons so well delivered that the soldiers took notes on the other side of the bars.

Ilario Da met Jorge Trujillo. He had been arrested on nothing more than a suspicion after a short strike in the factory where he worked. He spoke without recourse to metaphor or political theory, was neither eloquent nor talkative; he was humble, and did not see himself as a martyr. He disappeared soon after his arrival.

128

During a torture session, he had apparently confessed to knowing an MIR meeting place in a restaurant. The soldiers made him *porotear*, that is, he was to sit in the restaurant while they watched him from a few tables away, and discreetly point out the militants they were looking for. He was said to have ordered the best wine and the first dish on the menu, never looking up from his plate throughout the whole meal. When the waiter brought him the bill, he pointed to the soldiers disguised as civilians.

"These gentlemen are paying."

He was treated to his last dinner, and never seen again.

He got to know another prisoner, an old saltpeter miner, former Communist Party militant and great admirer of Recabarren, who went by the name of Don Hugo. He had made *miguelitos* in secret after his wife had forbidden him from getting involved in subversive activities. *Miguelitos* were twisted nails scattered on the road outside army barracks and police stations just before curfew, so that the only tires they punctured were those of surveillance patrols. The operation had gone wrong and he was now shaking his heavy handcuffs far from home, repeating: "You should always listen to your wife."

There was also a tall, strapping, brown-haired lad who said he had gone into business with his father to open a delicatessen. On the day of his arrest, he had paid one of his suppliers with a worthless check. With his head in his hands, he complained to himself.

"Whatever happens, even if I get out of here, I'll go back to prison for fraud."

Among them there was also a man of about forty. His name was Carmelo Divino Rojas and he was the ex-director of a review published in Concepción, which would be relaunched during his French exile by the journalist Armando Laberintos. One morning, soldiers came to his house to arrest him without a warrant or clear reason. Having decided to distance himself from the editorial board so as not to become caught up in politics, he was playing dominoes with his nephew. He was beaten, tortured, and when he asked for special treatment as a journalist at Villa Grimaldi, he was thrown into the same cell as everyone else.

Sometimes when he was overcome with rage, he couldn't stop himself saying out loud: "At least you all know why you're here. You're better at putting up with it, because you know what you're dying for. But I'm right-wing. I should be on the other side."

That day, a guard opened the door with a single kick.

"Who's talking?" he shouted.

Nobody moved.

"It's Carmelo, isn't it? Anyway, you can start saying your goodbyes. Your sentence has just been handed down: you're going to be shot."

They took him out. They bound him, put a black hood over his head and three guards on military service formed a firing squad. They raised their weapons. A fourth soldier read out the sentence and gave the signal. But instead of gunfire, there was a burst of laughter.

"He's fainted, the pussy!"

He had just experienced his first fake execution. He was still unconscious as they lifted him by the arms and took him to the interrogation room where he was tortured for an hour and made to swallow pentothal tablets as a form of truth serum. Shattered, he returned to the cell at dusk, almost lifeless, skinned alive. The others carefully lifted him onto the best bed.

When he could finally open his mouth, he muttered: "I'll never be free. I told them everything."

The prisoners and their torturers spent Christmas together, crammed inside an old tower which protruded from a thicket of willow trees. Around six in the evening, a guard brought a radio and tuned in to a football match between Huachipato and Unión Española. The volume was turned up high enough for the detainees to follow the game through the bars, and they began to compare the two teams, drawing out their discussion for as long as possible. Eventually the guards, bored and annoyed at having to work on Christmas Eve, made them tell jokes. Prisoner 392 was called upon first. In a small voice, with his eyes fixed on the ground, shaking all over, he told a lewd story about two priests at a urinal.

Next it was the turn of Ilario Da, who had been sitting in the corner in silence.

"I don't know any jokes, boss."

"Sing us something, then."

"I can't sing, boss."

The guard flew into a rage.

"We'll see if you can't sing, fucking communist."

He opened the door and everyone went rigid. The guard took Ilario Da by the arm. He was leading him out into the corridor when notes could be heard rising from the cell. A lone voice was singing a tango: "Volver" by Carlos Gardel. It was Carmelo Divino Rojas who, despite his fragile state, had brought his face to the bars to fill the other cells with song. Other voices joined his and, for a brief moment, Villa Grimaldi fell quiet to listen to the music, and just then it seemed to Ilario Da that they were not quite dead yet, that they could rise above the walls, the barbed wire and the blindfolds to dream of going home with furrowed brows, *volver con la frente marchita.*

Ilario Da was getting to his feet when amid the noise he heard a sharp cry, the sound of another fight, another voice, that of an old man being brought in. A guard was demanding he tell them where his son was hiding, but he was refusing and denying everything.

Several of them launched themselves at him with their bludgeons. Everyone realized his son must be Julián, an MIR leader who had been the subject of a countrywide manhunt since September 11. After half an hour, the old man was thrown into the hut and the door was angrily locked shut. He calmly took the seat nearest the door.

"Well," he said, "I wasn't planning to go out today anyway."

A ripple of awkward laughter went round the prisoners. But as it turned out, the old man had come bearing precious information.

"They say the French embassy is putting pressure on. They're preparing to release a *franchute*."

At first, Ilario Da didn't believe him. But shortly before nightfall, some nights later, he heard footsteps in the corridor.

The guard shouted from the door: "*Franchute*, get up."

On December 30, Ilario Da was let out of Villa Grimaldi, beaten and shorn, eight kilos lighter, scared by his sudden freedom, which seemed to him fragile and unfair. He was put in the back of an unmarked car, a Volkswagen K70, and Ilario Da wondered if this was not just another masquerade and he was going to be disappeared somewhere in the Atacama Desert. But the longer they drove, the more he heard the beeping horns of a big city and music coming from shops and buses, and he realized he was on Avenida O'Higgins, or perhaps Simón Bolívar, in the center of the capital.

As he was led out of the car, a gentle hand held on to his head to prevent him catching it on the doorframe. A woman walked him into a building and carefully pulled off the tape from his eyelids.

"Open your eyes slowly," she said. "It's very bright in here."

The world opened up before him again. He looked all around him and recognized the Fiscalía Militar. He was brought into a narrow anteroom at the top of a staircase. At the bottom were a series of offices, underground backrooms where men in ties sat tapping at typewriters. The young woman offered Ilario Da a cigarette, but he politely refused.

"I'm going to take the opportunity to give up smoking."

He entered an office furnished only with a table and, on the wall opposite, a blown-up photograph of Augusto Pinochet. Two clean-shaven men with gold buttons on their shirts read out his surname, rolled up their sleeves and asked him to recount every detail of the Friday afternoon in December when he had been arrested.

Disguising his hurt under cold formality, Ilario Da repeated his story that Hector Bracamonte was an activist militant of the extreme left who had hidden weapons inside the factory. Ilario Da was just a bourgeois with dual nationality, frivolous and superficial, young and stupid, who had somehow got caught up in the affair. When he had finished, one of the officers handed him the pen. Ilario Da did not have time to read back over his statement before signing it. As he left the room, he silently thought of Hector, who had spent his whole life trying to leave a legacy of easygoing respectability, and whose name would now appear, fifty-eight years later, among the orphans of history, when the only thing he had ever been guilty of was hunger.

Michel René

On May 21 of that year, old Lonsonier had celebrated his hundred-and-eighteenth birthday. Though the years of harvests had left him with a stoop, he was living proof that age was independent of the passage of time. Yet for the past several months, he had been unable to remember the name he had borne before moving to Chile. He was so used to his second identity he had forgotten the first. Amid the haze of his past, he could no longer picture the young winegrower he had once been, but his memory of the autumn afternoon when he met a fugitive from the capital remained crystal clear.

"His name was Michel René," he said, noting it down on a sheet of paper.

In 1873, a century before the Chilean *coup d'état*, old Lonsonier inherited a modest vineyard on the slopes of Lons-le-Saunier. He could never have imagined the sudden turn his life was about to take, leaving him washed up on the other side of the world just months later. At the end of August, his parents died of typhoid fever and, as if a curse had suddenly befallen his household, his vines also began to perish. Yet the collapse of the vineyard did not come entirely without warning. The savage aphid phylloxera had arrived in France from the United States several years earlier and established itself around Bordeaux and the Basque country. Lonsonier had heard about a certain Monsieur Delorme, a veterinarian from Arles who ran a vineyard in the south where all the leaves had turned yellow overnight. His plants had gone as pale as Andean gold, with galls blemishing their smooth surfaces. The wood dried out in the space of a few weeks. Each fallen vine released thousands of invisible aphids into the air which were carried on the rains from one estate to another, one root stock to the next, sweeping aside centuries of viticulture, only occasionally thwarted by spiders' webs woven between stems. Never had French winemaking witnessed a catastrophe of this scale: in the space of a few months, there was not a single vine left standing from Hérault to Alsace.

The local councils had the affected lands flooded, but it was soon clear the insects could survive in water. They applied chemicals which only accelerated the spread, killing neighboring apple trees and tomato plants in the process. Huge pyres of roots were burned, recalling the fires of the Paris Commune, and regional phylloxera commissions were sent out to spray the countryside with copper sulfate and carbon disulfide.

With his vineyard in the east of the country, Lonsonier initially profited from the rise in the price of wine. But one day when he was crossing his slopes, he caught an intensely sharp, bitter smell coming from the bark of his vines. Their leaves were all trembling, brown, studded with green buboes, covered in thousands of shells like so many drops of cyanide. He took some samples and discovered swarms of thirsty aphids tunneling inside every branch, coming and going through the sap, contaminating the land and ravaging the deep roots like an underground dictatorship.

Slicing the vines open with a pickax, he could see long lines of yellowish dots with his naked eye. Every plant was withered, every fruit wrinkled, and apart from a few old trunks still holding out, the whole plantation looked like an abandoned island kingdom. Little by little, Lonsonier's long rows of vines became a cemetery of diseased plants, a maze of sad and gloomy pathways, and within a few weeks his six hectares no longer produced a drop of wine.

He tried to fight back. He became a specialist in botany, consulted books on entomology and spent whole days inspecting bark under a magnifying glass. His war on aphids seemed to him an even higher and nobler cause than that of the Communards on the streets of Paris two years earlier. But at the end of these miserable harvests, when his biggest grape failed to reach the size of a peanut and his tallest plant was twelve centimeters high, Lonsonier was ruined. When, despite grafting healthy vine stocks and spraying the plantation with copper sulfate, it remained resolutely dead, he realized the battle was well and truly lost. Woodcutters collected wood from the estate to sell on to furniture manufacturers and instrument makers. Two months later, Lonsonier's vineyard had been turned into violins and bistro chairs.

Devastated, he let himself go. No sooner had he mourned the passing of his plants than the house fell into disrepair, becoming a bleak place where the ghosts of his parents still wandered dark corridors on lonely nights. Every room seemed as diseased as the vines. Damp frothed up the walls and the doors screamed on their rusty hinges. The shelves were covered in a snow of cobwebs. Rubbish was piled up in every corner of the kitchen. Flowers rotted in their pots and the mountains of dust had begun to house colonies of ants.

He was suddenly sure it was time for him to leave. For the past five years, winegrowers across France had been abandoning their estates to embark on the colonial adventure. The young and single ones without families to support or legacies to hand down were the first to board the ships for California, where it was said that the grapes of Napa Valley, northeast of San Francisco, might one day rival the great French wines.

He was so fixated on his imminent departure that when he got up to make a coffee one Thursday morning and realized the piles of rubbish had disappeared, he didn't give it a second thought. He was so tired he imagined he must be seeing things. Two days later, the tower of dirty dishes had been washed and put away. By the end of the month, there was not a single ant in the corners of the room, the cobwebs had been swept away, and the doors had been so well oiled they no longer made a peep.

"My God," he thought. "The ghosts are going to end up throwing me out."

One evening, before he had a chance to investigate these strange happenings, Lonsonier burst into his tool shed and discovered a man lying on a straw mattress, who immediately leapt to his feet.

The man looked scared, trembling, harmless. At first Lonsonier thought he had come from across the ocean, California perhaps, but the stranger knew nothing of America.

"I'm only running away from Paris, Monsieur."

The young man had fled the Commune in the middle of the *semaine sanglante*, escaping an unfair trial by hiding in a fruit cart.

"If you send me back, I'll be hanged," he said breathlessly.

His name was Michel René. All he had to his name was a brown coat with a velvet collar, red striped trousers and a checked cap. With his gray eyes and delicate nose, there was something rather feminine about his features. Had Lonsonier discovered a deserter sleeping in his shed a few months earlier, he would have gone straight to the police. But now that he was ready to go, leaving a ruined landscape behind him, he saw the fugitive as the savior of his vineyard.

The days that followed were taken up with planning his exile. All the imagination he had once put into resurrecting his land was now devoted to his leaving preparations. He was not trying to dodge the problems at hand but had lost all hope of extracting a single grape from this continent. He marked locations on maps, underlined sections of books on California and took notes on safely transporting vine stocks. In March, he sold half his furniture to pay for his ticket and, with his living room overflowing with bundles, boxes and trunks filled to bursting, there remained nothing to do but wait for the Cape Horner which would leave Le Havre for America in early spring.

Meanwhile Michel René calmly continued to rise while Lonsonier slept. He came out in the dark with a toolbox he had made himself, shyly floating about the corridors on the ground floor. He repaired wobbly shelves, swept the chimney and changed the oil in the lamps with such silent care and attention that Lonsonier came to think he must once have worked as a butler. Though Lonsonier tried to make conversation, Michel René remained reticent about his past. Hard farm labor, noisy jails and the difficulties of life on the move had made him so weary of his fellow man that this haven of ruined grapes, ghosts and leaky barrels seemed to him the perfect place to see out his days in silence. He spoke only to express gratitude or agreement. Past beatings had left him with a fearful demeanor. As Lonsonier watched him slip between the sparse rows of vines like a fleeting shadow or a timid cat, his anxious gait seemed to bear the secret mark of all the humiliations he had suffered.

A few weeks went by and on an overcast April 11, Lonsonier packed his last bag and dug up the single vine stock that had been left undamaged. He put thirty francs in his pocket along with a handful of oily earth. Having locked his cases, he broke open his barbotine money box to retrieve the last of his savings and headed towards the shed. Walking in to find Michel René hatless for the first time, with long hair held up in a black net, was a sight which would stay long in his mind. When he looked closely at Michel René's hips, he found they were fuller and more shapely than those of a man. A few buttons on his shirt were undone, revealing a rounded, youthful chest, and it was then that Lonsonier realized Michel René was a woman.

A Parisian in her thirties, she had joined a battalion of women at Place Blanche and later disguised herself as a man to fight on the barricades, wearing a semblance of a uniform and vermilion-striped trousers. Wounded and hunted, she took whatever hiding places fortune threw her way – inside mausoleums in cemeteries, former abattoirs and once even in Napoleon's imperial ateliers, where a mathematician by the name of Augustin Mouchot was building solar-powered engines. When she saw Lonsonier in the doorway, she blushed and threw a blanket over her shoulders to cover herself.

"Please don't send me away," she begged.

Hounded wherever she went, she had passed through every arrondissement and faubourg of Paris, defending her right to work, to education, to the civil code, to bear arms, and when an astonished Lonsonier asked her the reason for her cross-dressing, she replied with incredible assurance.

"Now I don't even have the right to be a woman."

Despite his surprise, Lonsonier did not reconsider his decision. He picked up his suitcase and gave her the keys to the house.

"If this estate is to be reborn," he told her, "let it be in the hands of a woman."

That same evening he left this land of chalk and cereal, morels and walnuts to board an iron ship at Le Havre bound for California. Since the Panama Canal was yet to open, he had to go the whole way round South America, traveling for forty days on a Cape Horner, aboard which two hundred men were crammed into cargo holds filled with caged birds, and the noisy fanfare was such that he didn't get a wink of sleep until the coast of Patagonia.

An accident of history made him disembark at Valparaíso on May 21. Without knowing it, he displayed courage as admirable as his son Lazare's, who would go to fight for France; bravery as exemplary as Margot's, who would fly high above the Channel; and resolve as proud as Ilario Da's, who would withstand torture in silence. And so it was that Lonsonier grafted the first root onto the trunk of descendants to come. Many years later as an old man living in Santiago with his family, he would continue to wonder if Michel René had really existed. But the day Lazare asked him which part of France his family came from, a distant memory of fugitives and aphids came rushing back to him, and he could only reply: "When you go to France, you'll meet your uncle. He'll tell you everything."

The name was carefully passed down the generations like a precious talisman. Which is why in December 1973, when Ilario Da disappeared in the Chilean prison system, Margot rued the year phylloxera had blighted French wine.

More than three weeks had passed since his arrest and the only thing they knew was that the junta was leaving many wrongs, crimes and misdemeanors unpunished, while keeping no record of the abuses it was committing. Sitting on a bench in the *carabineros'* office, Margot waited, silent and alone. She had written so many letters to the embassy, it was said the ink would not wash off her fingers. She had long since given up hoping Ilario Da would reappear and had taken to wandering about police stations as Michel René had once roamed the corridors of the house, staring at her gaunt, wizened, resigned face in the mirror, her features merging with those of the *desaparecidos* on the DINA lists. She spent her days seeking information in morgues and hospitals, returning home shocked by what she had seen: the horrifying proof that an entire generation was being massacred. In the gloom of her backyard, where she had tasted the dizzying wonders of science and an eagerness for love, she allowed herself to wither away like a lonely widow, her heart in tatters, barely even accepting visits from Bernardo Danovsky.

"You're the only one who understands me," she told him, "because you lost a child, too."

The old man brought her Jewish specialities like gefilte fish, beetroot soups, *bilkalej* and *verenike*, whose spiced aromas filled the empty rooms but could not mask the stench inside Margot's soul. He thought her skin was going the metallic color of a fuselage; her shoulders were hunched and her hands appeared to have shrunk; the pain of existence and anticipation of death hung over everything about her. He suggested she revive her pacifist meetings, change her furniture or plant some new flowers in the garden. But as Margot's despair pushed her to the brink of madness, she began searching for her son in prophetic dreams, in the divinations of tarot cards and symbols hidden in tea leaves and cigar ash, teaching herself all kinds of black magic. She was so utterly bereft that when she heard a knock at the door around three o'clock one Saturday, she didn't even bother to get up.

"That'll be the devil," she thought to herself.

The person who arrived in the garden having passed through the house without saying a word was a scrawny boy with trousers torn down to the knee and a piece of rope for a belt, a bloodstained shirt and a shaven head covered in black scars which he hid under a threadbare hat. The boy was no longer a boy, in fact, but the specter of the dictatorship– a crude, terrifying, gruesome metaphor for a murdered people. When she saw him, Margot thought he must have come to beg for a crust of bread, and when their eyes met, she didn't recognize her son, but took him for another ghost who had deserted an old colonial war.

"Life has sent me a second dead man," she said.

Ilario Da was so broken, humiliated and exhausted that Margot realized he had gone through a hell even bleaker than hers. Amid the confusion of his return, she did what all Lonsoniers had done: she went straight to run a bath, convinced by a long-held family belief that baths were among the only remedies for unhappiness. When Ilario Da undressed in front of her, she saw scars so deep and wounds so severe it looked as if an entire army had marched over him. In old Lonsonier's bathtub, she washed him with a knitted glove covered in linseed and spread a rosehip mask over his temples, leaving it to rest on his scars for three hours. Ice packs were placed on his head to bring down his fever. She applied a herbal poultice made with black hen's blood, as Aukan had used on Lazare's lung, because seeing him like this had brought her to the painful conclusion that all the men in the family suffered from the same ills and had to be cured with the same treatments.

After the bath he managed to drift off to sleep, but he woke with a start, shouting for help. He only calmed down when Margot came rushing in, keeping him in bed with infusions of liquid morphine. It was as if Hector Bracamonte's murder, the fear of being tortured again and the still-fresh injuries covering his body had brought back the same nightmarish images which had tormented Lazare after his brothers' deaths. And so in the days that followed Ilario Da's return, an awkward but beautiful bond was formed between mother and son, giving the former the strength to fight death, the latter to stave off madness. One night when he was rambling deliriously, puffy-eyed and frothing at the mouth, crying out Hector's name and talking about Carmelo Divino Rojas, Margot took a decision from which there was no going back.

"We're leaving this country in a week."

Since gaining official authorization to leave would be too lengthy a process, she took matters into her own hands. Making a decision as instinctive as that which once led her to join the Free French Forces on another continent, she tasked Aukan with speeding Ilario Da's recovery and headed to Tobalaba airdrome to resume building her plane. She gathered a group of old mechanics with whom she had kept in touch after the war, and was confident that her aircraft, hastily put together like Charles Lindbergh's *Spirit of St. Louis*, would be perfectly capable of crossing the cordillera.

Slumbering under the high nave of a hangar, her monoplane was surrounded by other machines resting in the chill, cathedral-like gloom. She visited the airdrome every day. Seized with a new burst of youth, she ordered the mechanics to regulate the instrument panel, reinforce the wings and replace the transmission, building a handmade monster and hoping for the best. By rekindling the crazy project which, despite her adolescent tenacity, had beaten her once before, she revived the brave warrior who had lain dormant inside her since her return from the front. When at last she tore herself away from her work, the plane was ready to go. Having studied a map of the cordillera in detail, Bernardo planned out the safest route.

"You'll see better by daylight," he said. "I'll clear the runway for you by dawn."

But Margot gave him a gently quizzical look. She knew that her giddy ambitions meant she was always destined to fly in the face of danger. She had been waiting so long for this flight, had sacrificed so much, inspired by a messianic calling, that her voice remained perfectly steady as she objected: "They'll see us better by daylight."

For the first time since they had known one another, she spoke to him sharply and firmly. As she fixed him with a fiery stare, he dared not contradict her.

"We'll take off tonight," she added.

Neither the caution counseled by friendship, nor the walls of ice ahead, nor the traps laid by nostalgia could put her off. She went home, emptied her room, gathered her meager savings in a little box and uprooted the vine from her garden, weighed down with tattered leaves, as reverently as her grandfather Lonsonier had planted it many years before. She told Ilario Da to slather his body in grease and onion skins, to mitigate the effects of low oxygen, and hid an ax under her seat, more out of superstition than necessity.

At ten o'clock that night Margot and Ilario Da left Tobalaba along a runway Bernardo had lit for them. They spiraled high towards the east at four thousand meters altitude and set a course for the Andes. Within half an hour, they were in the mountains.

Though she could not see it, Margot's calculations suggested the volcano of Tupungato was soaring up ahead of them in the central ramparts, where a narrow crescent of snowy valleys formed a saddle between the mountains. She stared into the crests and cols of Aconcagua, picturing them as she had seen them on maps, laid out beneath her feet in rocky hollows, giant craters and lakes beginning to thaw. The gaps between the peaks were few and winding, the walls high as a fortress, so that with every move she made, Margot felt her wing tips were grazing the skin of the rocks.

After forty-five minutes in the air, she calculated they must be around halfway across the chain. While she kept a close eye on their flight path, Ilario Da swung between fear and sleep, still fragile after his torture, leaning against the window in stunned silence. Around eleven o'clock, the plane was rocked by strong turbulence. It seemed invisible forces were drawing her towards the rock face and she narrowly avoided striking an overhang, but managed to right the plane. Over and over again she thought she would founder, buffeted by the ferocious Andean winds, but each time she miraculously escaped. While she was being jolted, a powerful, more sustained wave propelled her into a column of air so forceful the plane was tossed about like a dead leaf. Feeling frightened, Margot made out an escarpment between two walls of rock and shook herself free. But no sooner had she entered this corridor than she became trapped in a funnel, the narrow passage creating a series of whirlwinds drawing her downwards.

Margot cut the engine and went into freefall. Seeing a terrace in the distance, about four hundred meters long and wide enough to land on, she turned the plane's wheels towards the plateau. Carefully navigating between the humps and rocks, she managed to make a sharp landing on a blanket of powdery snow. A noisy clash racked the plane. It jumped, slid, lurched forward, narrowly avoiding a ravine, then came slumping to a stop. Margot immediately let go of the controls and stepped out of the cockpit. Everywhere in the mirrored, wind-whipped summits, the whistling ivory peaks around them, a giants' cemetery spread out as far as the eye could see. She inspected their surroundings and, while the mountain opening was narrow, she was relieved to see that the platform was on a slight incline pointing towards a passage wide enough for the wings to get through.

"We can use this as a springboard to lift off again," she smiled.

They were at four thousand meters altitude and the temperature was minus ten, but remembering Los Cerrillos, the port of London and the German fighters over the Channel, Margot's muscles were pumped up with courage. She studied the terrain, the state of her fuselage and landing gear, circling her aircraft like a mechanic in a hangar. In a sudden burst of inspiration, she began twisting ropes of leather, hammering sheets of metal and straightening the tail wheel, while giving orders to Ilario Da to remove any unnecessary parts in order to lighten the plane. Their hands turned blue and their noses bled. The fog was so cold they couldn't feel their feet for two days. The radiator pipes froze and cracked, and they had to use all the trousers in their suitcases to block up the holes. Boldly, madly, filled with belief in a plane whose every inch she knew like an extension of her own body, Margot calculated it would take to the air if it was launched from the slope.

"It's our only hope," she told Ilario Da.

She sat at the controls and turned on the engine. Ilario Da pushed the plane slowly towards the top of the slope. The wheels slid on the ice and the plane quickly picked up speed as it hurtled downhill. Ilario Da jumped in the back and, thrilled by the adventure, Margot accelerated at the jumping-off point, pressing the thrust lever. She arched the plane to the brink of destruction, began to climb and build up speed, flying blindly into the winds and, using the same air current which had caused her to fall, headed out towards the valley and Argentina beyond.

At midnight, Ilario Da and Margot reached Mendoza. Those who remembered that night would speak of seeing a strange plane emerging from a white sky and a long-haired woman and shaven-headed man stumbling out, their frozen feet preventing them from walking.

"How wonderful," Margot gushed breathlessly. "I should have done this all my life."

*

One January Tuesday, the liner *Sainte-Croix* set sail from Buenos Aires bound for Saint-Nazaire. But Margot was not on board. She stood motionless on the Argentine quay, staring at an imaginary point on the horizon, knowing that nothing awaited her in Europe but a fickle swell of memories.

"I can't do it," she said. "I can't live on a continent where I've died once before."

She pulled from her bag a stack of old, dog-eared, yellowed papers bound with string to make a notebook, and slid them inside her son's suitcase.

"I saved them from the red box," she told him. "Make something of them."

Then the boat lifted its gangways with white snakes of rigging and Ilario Da hurried aboard. Theirs was a goodbye without words or gestures. Neither of them waved from a distance. Margot's eyes misted over as she felt a turmoil which would never leave her. With trembling legs and a still swollen face, Ilario Da did not have the strength to promise he would return. Whenever he thought of her, it would always be like this: standing in a fishing port, carrying the exhaustion of a half-century's battles on her shoulders.

On the Río de la Plata, the last Lonsonier's exile was beginning. Ilario Da's fellow passengers appeared carefree, seemingly unaware of the dictatorship, and it was absurd to him that these families were calmly going about their lives on the same vessel that was saving him from death. But the hardest thing was the certain knowledge that his departure would pave the way for thousands of other young Chileans who would be rushing to board ships, cram onto planes and cross the cordillera on muleback behind him, who sat waiting in cold prisons for rubber stamps from foreign administrations, customs clearances and safe conduct papers allowing them to go to faraway places where no one would understand what they had been through.

At the time, France was a safe haven, welcoming political refugees from all around the world. Yet the possibility of giving up the fight, of not going back to Chile, never crossed his mind. There was no interest, dignity or bravery in a life outside political combat. His comrades without dual nationality had been left behind in Santiago. Ilario Da felt the injustice of this deeply, and his return was a foregone conclusion. He had no idea he would in fact stay in Paris for more than ten years. He did not know he would move into a narrow attic room, without condors or araucarias, where he would write the story of his torture, or that many years later at a football match in the Bois de Vincennes, he would meet a courageous woman named Venezuela, who had come from a land of orchids and oil, of boats laden with spices and sadness, and who would guide him towards another revolution.

Strolling the deck during the empty hours of the crossing, his mind was set alight with thoughts of his past. He took the notebook made by Margot out of his little suitcase and began to write. It was more than a simple compulsion to bear witness; his need to put pen to paper came from much further back, as if resurging from the well of nostalgia, from the days when Aukan had taught him marvelous stories of young girls born from fire, and giants turning into wooden statues. As he tried to put his past behind him, Hector's face seemed to emerge, clear and calm, from the limpid waters of the sea, the memory of him closer the further the ship traveled from shore. And so the day old Lonsonier had first crossed the Atlantic, he had merely placed the first piece on the chessboard of migrations his family would carry on after him. One hundred years, two world wars and a dictatorship later, here was his great-grandson taking the same route in reverse, and perhaps in another half-century, another exile would come to be added, another tendril in a boundless jungle of quests, sorrows and births.

It was only when the French coast came into view that the country really began to exist for Ilario Da. He stepped off the boat with thirty francs in one pocket and a vine stock in the other. He had nothing to his name besides a gray suit and a pair of boots. In his suitcase was the manuscript of the Chilean front. When he reached the immigration desk, he had to join a long queue.

An hour later, a customs officer asked him: *"Nom?"*

The enigmatic question awakened something in his memory, a deep echo of the distant past. Though he was a long way from the dictatorship and the Chilean *carabineros*, he was struck with the fear they might come looking for him across the ocean. He thought of several possible aliases, pseudonyms, code names, but the only one which came to his lips was the name all his ancestors had repeated before him.

"Michel René," he said.

The woman did not look up. With a careless gesture of her hand which, in a single line, would rechristen the entire family tree after him, she noted on the form:

Michel René.

MIGUEL BONNEFOY was born in France in 1986 to a Venezuelan mother and a Chilean father. His two previous novels, *Octavio's Journey* and *Black Sugar*, have sold more than thirty thousand copies each in France and have been translated into several languages. In 2013 Bonnefoy was awarded the Prix du Jeune Écrivain. *Heritage* has received widespread critical acclaim in France, including being short-listed for the Prix Femina, Grand Prix de l'Académie française, and the Prix Goncourt.

EMILY BOYCE is an editor and translator based in London. Her translations include works by Antoine Laurain, Pascal Garnier, and Laurent Gaudé, and two previous novels by Miguel Bonnefoy. She was short-listed for the 2016 French-American Foundation Translation Prize for her translation of Éric Faye's *Nagasaki*.